acceleration

a novel

by S. N. Hayes

imperceptions

First Printing 2020
Second Edition 2025
Print ISBN: 978-1-990467-25-7
Hardcover ISBN: 978-1-990467-26-4
Ebook ISBN: 978-1-990467-27-1

Cover, Book Layout, Print, and eBook design
by East Coast Designs.
www.eastcoastdesigns.ca

Edited by Macie Gardner

acceleration

imperceptions

Imperceptions Press
Oromocto, New Brunswick
www.imperceptions.com

Acknowledgements

Thank you to Macie for your wonderful editing! You went above and beyond. I really appreciate it.

I'd also like to thank all of the people who encouraged me along the way—even when my writing wasn't great. Especially Judy, my high school librarian, and my high-school teacher, Tracey, who ironically taught math yet suggested books for me!

Thanks to my friends, family, my mom Michelle, and my dad Roddie who supported me even when I was an annoying brat.

To Preston—because you always believe I can accomplish whatever I set my mind to. Thank you for putting up with me.

*For all those who believed in me, and especially
for all those who didn't.*

acceleration

Prologue

It's stupid, absolutely pointless. The risk is too great, too high. We deserve everything that goes wrong. Every car crash. Every arrest. We know that we're not perfect, and that's okay.

We live for the asphalt.

We justify it, because for us, there's no other way to live.

The adrenaline high is too strong. The humming motor of our cars. The scent of gasoline as it trickles to our nostrils on a hot summer night.

We're alive.

Intoxicated.

Even if it only lasts a short while, even if we lose it all. It's worth it.

Not that there's much else left to lose without this feeling. We're nothing without the vibrations.

Without this speed. We're lurching forward toward

nothing in particular. Moving, like the ocean, because sheer force and nature pulls us along.

Fighting our desire is like moving against the current.

Sure, we might still drown, and whether we win or lose, the outcome is the same.

Regrets are pointless. There is only you and the car.

Chapter 1: Amanda

Amanda closes the door on her Subaru WRX with a soft thud. She presses the lock button on her key and places it in her pocket.

She has no business being here, and yet that doesn't stop her; her Dolce and Gabbana flip-flops clacking against the hot summer asphalt. She questions her choice of footwear, down to the pink bottoms and gold tops. Girls like her—the ones who wear shoes like this—shouldn't be in the warehouse district at 9pm on a Friday night. She should go to a club or pick classes for a fall semester at the college she dropped out of.

A loud thump distracts her from her looming self-doubt and replaces her imposter syndrome with raw, tangible fear.

Two men in their late twenties are facing each other. One has a tire-iron in his right hand. The other, for some unfathomable reason, is laughing.

"I didn't mean to hit your car, bro," one man says to the other, shrugging his shoulders.

An orange '67 Dodge Charger had flung its door into a 2014 Shelby 500.

There's a clear dent in the Mustang's door.

"You didn't mean to? Then why did you park so close?" he says, his voice getting louder with each word.

He lunges at him, narrowly missing the second man's temple.

"Jeez, chill out. It's just a fucking dent."

"A dent? This paintwork costs more than your entire car!"

Amanda half-expects somebody to pull a gun. Instead, an engine revs in the distance.

"Let's race this out," the angry man says, pointing. "If you lose, you're paying for the bodywork—and you're buying me a new TV too."

They agree. Amanda lets out her breath, glad that she isn't about to witness a murder. The tension in her body eases slightly as the men retreat to their cars.

The cars start, and within moments, they're revving their engines and readying for the challenge. She hurries to the side to ensure that she doesn't become the victim of the man that, just moments ago, was ready to create blood-stained artwork on the pavement.

She nearly jumps out of her skin when she feels a tap on her shoulder. She twists, mentally preparing herself for the worst even though her rational brain isn't sure what the worst would even be.

Andy, a New Yorker she met when her mother forced

her to spend summers there as a kid, is standing beside her.

"What are you doing here?" she says, a little too shocked to sound polite.

"What are you doing here?" he says and then laughs, more jeering than insulted.

"It doesn't matter," she says. How can she explain to Andy why she's there when she's not so sure it's a superb idea?

She tries to focus on the cars half-heartedly because she's not vying for a winner.

"Here to pick up a street racer?" he asks, and she visibly winces.

"Definitely not," she says, her tone defensive.

For most of the race, the two cars disappear. She and Andy are silent for a while, content to await the cars coming back as they take in the scene that surrounds them. Cars are in every corner of the parking lot. Aside from two streetlamps, most of the lights are coming from the headlights on the cars. Some of the cars are decorated with colored lights and many varieties of music play from speakers inside them. The music muffles together into one thumping bass-beat.

The two cars return, the owner of the Mustang trium-phant. He exchanges money with the loser, and his bad mood seems replaced by a winner's high.

She watches as two cars pull up to the start/finish line hastily drawn with sidewalk chalk; the finish line is more of a finish zigzag.

A green '97 Supra and a black 66' Dodge Charger are

side by side. The custom green paint job is vaguely familiar.

One driver revs his engine, and the other driver squeals the wheels of his car.

"The Dodge is a powerful car," Andy says.

Amanda had almost forgotten Andy was there. She glances at him and shakes her head in disagreement.

"I don't know. The Supra looks nice," Amanda says as she crosses her arms, a slight breeze chilling her arms.

"It's not how a car looks. It's what's on the inside," he says, pointing at the cars. "The Dodge is classic."

"Sure, but it's muscle versus import," she says. "I'm not even sure why they're bothering."

"Well, why not?" Andy asks, and she shrugs.

One of the cars revs its engine, the other responds accordingly; one car purrs, the other roars. The cars jolt forward. They take a minute to accelerate, but once they do, they whip out of sight.

She's not exactly sure what she expected—just being here is enough to make her hands shake.

"Did you bet on the race, Amanda?"

"Honestly, I didn't even consider betting," she says. Andy's question brings back her self-doubt. "I'm saving money for my car."

"Oh?" he asks, his eyes still scanning the distance for the cars.

She bites her lip. She can feel her stomach gurgling from anxiety and fear of Andy's judgement.

"I want to race," she says, still timidly, testing how it sounds out loud.

"It'll be hard as hell to get them to take you seriously," he says, his attention only half on her.

"I know that," she says. It doesn't change the pent-up desire that's been boiling over for the last few years. Even if it's the worst idea she's ever had, she wants it too bad to forget about it.

"It's kind of boring waiting for them to get back," he says. "I'd rather be racing."

The last of the sun is disappearing, the heat from earlier replaced by a sudden chill.

After a couple minutes, the sound of screeching tires pierces through the night. The two cars spin around the corner. The Charger has two smashed headlights, and the Supra is unscathed.

The Supra is also a good half a second ahead and flashes across the chalk line.

The driver of the Charger is beating his fists on the steering wheel, and her stomach knots.

"I guess you lost your money," she says.

"Nah, I bet on the Supra."

Amanda's eyes narrow. "You bet on the driver you thought would lose?"

"I may think Ben has a good enough car, but I hate him," Andy says as he shrugs.

He places his hand on her shoulder for a moment. She wonders if she should brush him off, but he smiles.

"Listen, it was great catching up, but it's time for me to drive," he removes his hand from her shoulder. "Let me know when you're ready to race. I want to see what you can do."

She nods and smiles too.

Andy turns toward the cars, and within a few moments, she loses sight of him. Instead, she catches sight of the Supra's driver. She takes a much-needed deep breath. Of course the Supra had won—Ryder is an amazing driver. He always has been.

Ryder grins at the crowd, and a couple of girls immediately bring him drinks and fawn over him. Guys who had been recording the race congratulate him, and one pats him on the back. He's a champion, and by the look on his face, he knows it.

The other driver is ushered away. A few wise friends keep the two from interacting. By the looks of the headlights, it's a necessary precaution. Ryder may have won, but he didn't do so without playing dirty.

Ryder looks tougher than she remembers. His face is older and stronger. He was never weak, but he's no longer a rebellious kid fresh from high school.

He notices her staring.

"Amanda, is that you?" he asks, calling out to her.

She could walk away and pretend she didn't hear him. Or she could suck it up. Coming here was bound to dredge up the past. Might as well face it sooner rather than later. Even though she'd hoped for the latter.

She was supposed to meet with her friend from college, Natalie, but she hasn't seen her anywhere.

She swallows her breath. Amanda's never been afraid of anybody, ever. Why does she feel so freaked out by Ryder?

It's not long before he walks over to her. She hasn't seen him in four years. Her hands shake slightly, so she places them in her back pockets, determined not to let on that she's anxious.

"So, what're you doing here, Amanda?"

Lie. That's her first instinct. Lie, walk away, and never come back. She could go home and pretend this never happened.

"I guess I missed this," she says.

She missed the cars, anyway. The men that drive them is another story.

"You missed watching street racing?" Ryder asks, narrowing an eyebrow.

He's still glowing from his win.

"Not just street racing—cars, racing, the thrill," she stops herself to take a quick breath.

He nods slightly, as though he understands, and looks back at the two cars that have pulled up to the line.

"Connors isn't going to beat Ben until he gets rid of that little crap Mitsubishi."

"Ben? Is that the guy whose car you decimated?"

Ryder smirks, his eyes animated by the mention of his win. "Yeah, that'd be him."

"You're lucky he didn't punch you," she says.

"Funny he didn't try," Ryder says, and he laughs for a moment then continues, "Andy's a good driver, but his car just isn't good enough to win; not that I'd mind if Ben lost again," he says, his eyes on her.

"Why, what's wrong with Ben?" Amanda turns her

attention back and forth between the car and Ryder but only glances at Ryder briefly between speaking.

She can't look at him too closely without thinking about the past.

"Everybody here is competition," he says. His teeth grit together.

She needs to get far away from Ryder before she reconsiders every life choice that led her to the parking lot.

"I should go; the girl I was meeting up with isn't here,"

"Yeah, you better run home to your mansion," he says before laughing at his own pathetic joke. She shouldn't be surprised he has turned so cold, so fast.

"I live in my garage now."

"Why?" he says, his eyes narrowing, and his shoulders pulled back as he speaks.

"I want to race," she says. She stops her hands from trembling and straightens her spine.

He laughs again. Right in her face.

"You don't have to be a total asshole about it," she says. Her hands are no longer shaking.

"Sorry," he says, staring at her. "I just didn't think you were the type."

"Type? And what type are you?" she asks, her voice snapping.

"I don't know," Ryder says. His nose scrunched. "I guess I'm the type that can spill motor oil on my shirt and not break into tears."

"Don't be afraid because you know I'll eventually get better than you, Ryder." She probably won't be, but she doesn't care.

"Go ahead and get your car, and we can test whether or not you actually belong here."

"Belong here? It's a back street, not the Winston Cup," she huffs out a breath after speaking. Fuck him.

"Exactly," he says and then smirks. "We don't have safety precautions and white flags."

"I'll risk it. Why do you care? Are you worried about me?"

"No," he says. His eyes move down her body. "I'm just worried you'll break a nail."

Amanda turns on her heel, unable to handle any more of Ryder's bullshit.

"I'm not going to be breaking anything that's not on your car," she says as she walks off, too angry to face him.

"Go ahead and try," he calls out to her backside as she leaves.

Chapter 2: Ryder

He watches Amanda walk towards her car. The tiny blonde girl wants to race? Yep. Her failure is certain. Her reasons for racing, less so. Of course, she'd choose a Subaru. The sleek body and the blue tones—very likely that she had chosen the car simply for its curb appeal. Only a scoff could manage to convey the emotion that surfaced at the idea of Amanda becoming a street racer.

Whatever reason she has to be here, it doesn't matter. She's stirred up feelings he forgot he had. His anger toward Jordie intensifies. Vodheo causes nothing but problems.

He leans against his Green '97 Toyota Supra. Since he's won, girls seem to be coming closer to him. Everybody wants to be with the winner. He's not against their fawning, but it's not something that will last. As soon as he loses, he'll be replaced by the next winner.

"Was that who I think it was?"

Like clockwork. Where there's Amanda, there's Jordie. The two had been intertwined for years, and yet, nothing has changed.

The hairs on the back of his neck stand up at the sound of Jordie Vodheo's voice. For the past 5 years, he hasn't found another guy that has come closer to being his greatest rival—smug, irritating, and a boundless egomaniac.

"Yes," he says.

"What is she doing here?"

He shrugs.

Jordie leans against the Supra too. He takes a deep breath, pressing his tongue against his cheeks. Don't hit him. Don't hit him. He's not worth it.

"I haven't seen her in years," Jordie says.

Neither had he. And yet, here they are, talking about it. The last thing he wants to do.

"Good luck telling Brooke that you saw her," Ryder says. He wants Jordie to go away. "Or you could always not tell her and lie."

He wants to make Jordie feel uncomfortable.

"No matter what I do, I'm sure it's going to be thrown back in my face."

"Probably."

Like he cares what happens to Jordie.

Jordie, walking around the Supra, runs his fingers across the side of the car.

Ryder growls as he speaks, "Do you mind?"

"Come on, let's race."

He's already won once tonight. He should stop and go

home. Take home his victory and sleep easy.

"Alright," he says before thinking harder. Victory is one thing, but walking away from Jordie, that's an impossibility.

Jordie smirks.

He wants to slap him across the face. He'll have to settle for causing damage to The Judge. Jordie's GTO is the car of a classic-attention seeker. Everything he does is for show. He couldn't have a modern car. No, it had to be something that was a legend.

"Let's go," Ryder says. He'll beat this asshole, and then he can go home and have a beer. No triumph is really enough until it involves seeing Jordie flat on his ass.

Chapter 3: Natalie

The subtle difference between the shaking rumble of her Chevelle and the roar of a Dodge Challenger may not be what most of the girls at the race are thinking about, but for her, the machinery itself is more enthralling than any of the drivers. Even Jordie's GTO has its own specific sound, so intricate that the engine itself is speaking its tale. Jordie, though, seems to only be saying "Look at me," as he flexes his muscles in front of the girls watching him in awe.

In awe of what? She's not sure. As far as she can tell, there's not a lot going on in his head, but he wins enough races that the girls keep flocking. They try with Ryder too, but he doesn't seem as interested. He gets enough girls, which is clear by the slow click of the front door in the middle of the night, but he never takes them home; he always just leaves and then comes back in the early hours of the night, and they never discuss it.

In fact, she never brings anybody home either. Especially not Ben. Ryder surely knew something about their tumultuous affair, but he never asks questions. As far as either of them is concerned, their love lives are completely off topic. She's glad because there's not a lot to say about her relationship with Ben. She's not even sure if she ever loved him or if it was a delayed response to circumstances. Either way, she's determined that whatever it is stays over.

She met Ben at the races during her first year of classes. She was surprised to learn that he was attending the same school. He had even convinced her, rather passionately, that she should take a political science class. She dropped the intro within the first 6 weeks. Ben tried to explain to her the systems of government, even went as far explaining that all of life was political, but she informed him that she wanted to build things, not analyze people. Machines were always easier to understand—at the very least they could be used for scraps when things completely disintegrated.

"Yes, but machines can't do this," he had said, leaning in and kissing the nape of her neck as they huddled together in the back of the campus library, not even pretending to study on the leather sofa barely hidden by two rows of books.

She presses her hand to her neck, almost feeling the ghost of the kiss. She briefly closes her eyes but only lets the moment last a few seconds before opening them and removing her hand. The memory of her relationship with Ben has been marred too much to think only of the good, and just then, the same miserable grayness overcomes her. She has to make a choice to either cry or stop thinking of him completely.

It would be easier to let go if Ben would just stop calling her or cornering her at races.

Ryder, just having finished a race, curses, and she looks up, quick to ask, "What's wrong?"

He groans and then lifts the hood, moving back so that she can examine the damage for herself. He might have won, but the car itself is sending its own message: too much, too fast. She sighs and starts digging around, examining the problem and making a few adjustments, nodding for Ryder to start the car. When she finishes, everything seems normal, and he nods at her and says, "Gracias."

"You're welcome," she responds in English. Despite their Mexican heritage, she usually only speaks Spanish when she's drunk—or pissed off.

Ryder probably could have fixed the car himself, but he insists that she's a mechanical genius, and it's not like she's ever disputed the title. Something about machines, really seeing what makes them work, pulling them apart and then finding where the pieces fit back together, has always been comforting for her. Once as a kid, she had completely decimated the family lawn tractor which was particularly frustrating for her father because it was during an unseasonably wet summer when the grass had sprung out of control. He had to replace the tractor.

Eventually, as a teenager, he had given her his beat-up Chevelle with the promise that she'd stop taking things apart and would dedicate that attention to the car. If he knew she had eventually started street racing, he probably would have let her keep tinkering with lawnmowers.

The Chevelle SS to the right of Ryder's Supra sits pristine. The bodywork Ryder helped with, but the engine she had rebuilt herself, probably using too many of her summer paychecks. The car—blue paint, racing stripes, and humble engine growl—had made everything worth it, and Natalie knew she was capable of going fast. It would have been a shame not to use her.

"Do you think I should race again tonight?" Ryder asks.

Natalie shakes her head. "Give the car a break," she says, "or else you might regret it."

He nods and says, "Yeah, I figured. Unless you want to let me use the Chevelle..."

She throws a dagger look at him. Nobody uses the Chevelle. Ever.

Ryder laughs and shakes his head. "Don't worry, it was a joke."

She sighs with relief and smiles. Just because he's family doesn't mean she's going to trust him with her car. She grazes her fingertips over the Supra, thinking about her own race and how she'd managed to win despite the other driver having a fully restored Charger.

Chapter 4: Ben

"$80, and it's yours," Ben says.

The man in front of him has shifty eyes. He reaches into his pocket to retrieve his cash. Ben assumes the money was obtained from gambling or stolen. Oh well.

"That's $5 increase from last week," the man named Carl says, his voice screeching.

"Drugs are expensive. Get over it." Ben says. "I don't make the prices; I just collect the money."

"They're not usually this expensive."

"Listen, if you don't want it, go somewhere else. It's $80 or nothing." Ben shakes his head; his eyes are narrowed, but his breathing is steady.

"Fine, but I'm going to be having a word with your boss about this." The guy takes the money out. It's a wad of scrunched up bills. He clenches them in tangled hands.

"You're going to complain to Edge?"

Ben's boss, or supplier, is one of the few people that makes even him uneasy. Ben never asks questions past 'How much do we sell it for?'. Edge has a reputation, and most of it involves missing person's reports.

"Oh," the man says, and then pauses as he considers Ben's words. His face twists into worry and then back to irritation. "Well, you're not going to get very much business if you keep raising your prices like this."

"Yeah, yeah, Carl. I'll let the boss know that the drug business is going to suffer because of the economy; maybe he can start peddling hot dogs."

Ben takes the money and slams the drugs into Carl's hand.

"Don't take too many—or do. I don't really care," he says.

The other man shuffles out of the room. Ben rolls his eyes, shaking his head. Sadly, this is just a regular part of his morning. He probably shouldn't have let Carl know where he lives, but he has a hard time caring. Maybe Carl will come back with a baseball bat or gun. At least then his misery would be cut short.

Leaning back in his chair, Ben sips a lukewarm cup of coffee. It's cheap and possibly decaf. He cringes at the taste, having to lick his lips to handle the bitterness. Regardless, he takes several quick gulps of the coffee. He checks his phone for the tenth time. He has a few messages from questionable people but none from anyone he actually wants to talk to. One person in particular is always on his mind. It doesn't matter, though, because she wants to talk to him about as much as he wants to spend the day in his apartment.

"Good morning," Ruth says as she walks out from the bedroom. "Who was here?"

"A client."

"Oh" she says, and reaches for Ben's coffee, taking a sip for herself. "Eww, that's disgusting." She puts the cup beside him, her eyes hovering over his phone.

Ben clicks the lock button and puts it beside the coffee. His nostrils flare, and he sighs. The last thing he needs is Ruth reading his messages over his shoulder. She knows he's a drug dealer; what more does she want?

Ruth is about 5'3 and has medium length brown hair. Instead of clothes, she has a red housecoat on. Her eyes move toward the bedroom, and she subtly licks her lips. She's kind of mousy but inarguably attractive, the house-coat perfectly settling over her small frame.

"Yeah, good morning. There's more coffee in the pot. Get your own."

Her eyes narrow, and her lips purse. Instead of commenting on his rudeness, her face softens, and she walks across the room to the counter, pouring her own cup of coffee in a grimy mug. "Do you want to do something today? A movie maybe?"

"I can't. I've got to go out," he says before yawning. "I have to work."

"Oh," Ruth says, her voice wispy.

Ben ignores it. He has little to no time for her. Ruth's always trying to act like they're friends or even a couple. He doesn't want her to get the wrong idea. She's just some girl that happens to be sleeping in his bed—and occasionally with him. That's it. He's already let her crash at his apartment, have half his bed, and eat whatever she can find in the cupboards.

Ben gets up from his chair and gives Ruth a once-over. Annoying or not, he can't deny that she looks sexy in her satin house coat. It fits tightly around her chest and is cut low on her thighs. He takes a deep breath and ignores the urge to push her into the bedroom. He has other stuff to do.

"I'll be back tonight," he says.

"Oh," Ruth sounds discouraged. He resists the urge to bang his head against the wall. "What time?"

"I don't know, Ruth." He grabs a sweater and quickly goes for the door, slamming it behind him. It's hard avoiding the sex, but it's not worth the agony of listening to Ruth whine.

Once on the street, he shivers slightly. It's unnaturally cool for June. A breeze pushes past him and tosses crumpled newspapers across the pavement.

At the race the night before, Ben lost quite a bit of money. What annoys Ben most is the back bumper of his car being left behind.

He doesn't really need money, but he does need his car. He isn't as die-hard as the other racers, but he's not thrilled to have his car fucked up.

Groaning, Ben checks his phone once more. He has about an hour before he has to get back to Edge and give him the profits. Edge always takes part of his cut mid-week.

Before putting his phone away, Ben looks at a picture of his ex-girlfriend that he'd taken before she discovered that she deserved better. Staring at her face to start his day is a desperate addiction. He should probably delete the picture. He's tried before, but every time he gets even close to the delete button, he freezes and closes the app instead. She may not be coming back for good, but he can't let go either.

***

Ten minutes later, Ben slinks into the back booth of a diner. The coffee is only a little better than what he has at home, but at least it has caffeine. Besides, there's less bitterness. Unlike his fridge at home, the cafe is fully equipped with milk. He never thinks to buy groceries. The least Ruth could do is go shopping.

He's glad to be away from her. Ever since she'd used him as a get-out-of-her-life card, she'd been obsessive and clingy. It was supposed to be a couple nights on his couch after she came in from New York. Days quickly became three months.

Ben watches a skinny waitress with a blonde bun come over to take his order. She looks tired, and her apron is full of grease.

"Can I get you something?" she says, approaching the table. Her face slumps when she locks eyes with him.

Ben comes in here every day. That doesn't mean the waiting staff likes him.

"Same as usual, Daphne. Piece of pie, another coffee, and a little bit of you," he says as he winks at her. He knows he makes her stomach churn, but he still can't resist. Daphne is an easy target, and since she had passed him off as a bad guy, he is happy to deliver.

Daphne sighs and takes down his order, probably leaving out the part about casual hate sex.

"One of these days I'm going to report you to the manager," Daphne says.

"You wouldn't. You like my smile," Ben says as he plays with the saltshaker and pours a little bit of salt out on the table.

Daphne's eyes turn a dark shade of grey.

"Will that be all?" she asks, her voice exasperated.

"Yes, please," he says as he continues to spread the salt around. Daphne turns on her heel, hightailing it back to the kitchen. She's probably debating whether or not she can quit her job and get away with it. Or just as likely, she's wondering if she can get away with murder.

Ben makes no attempt to hide that he's watching her as she walks towards the kitchen. She has a skinny body and droopy eyes that show she works at least one other job. She isn't exactly his type, but he admires a girl who is willing to work her way through life.

Daphne approaches slowly with his pie and his coffee. "You didn't say what kind, so I brought you apple," she says, her tone flat and cool.

"Apple'll do," he says, and he takes a bite and gives her a thumbs up, talking with his mouth full to say, "It's not bad."

"Good, I'm glad," she says as her teeth grate together, her jaw clenching.

He smiles as she walks away. He's pretty sure that she'll be talking behind his back to the other waitresses about how he's the spawn of Satan.

Chapter 5: Natalie

"How did you start street racing?" Amanda asks as Natalie works on installing some of the latest parts that arrived.

It started when she was young. Go-karts at an amusement park that her father would take her to—he never encouraged them, but the two kids, her and Ryder, were relentless.

They couldn't even go swimming without one of them being at risk for drowning. One time, and she's a little ashamed she's proud of this, she managed to flip him over and hold his taller, 2-year older body underwater for almost a minute.

"Ryder and I've always liked cars. I guess all it really took was having the cars and wanting to race them," she says. "It's not that hard to find street racers. Find a guy who knows a guy, and you're ready to go."

Amanda nods, "Who'd you know?"

"Ryder worked at a garage for a while. The garage owner, Eric, bet him an aftermarket turbo kit if he could win a race."

"What's a turbo kit?" she asks.

Natalie sighs. "Are you sure you should be driving this car?" she asks, running her fingers on the front bumper.

Amanda shrugs and says, "I just want to drive the car; what goes into it, that's up to you. Just make it fast."

"The turbo makes the car faster by forcing more air into the combustion chamber," she says. "I went with him. I was already fixing the Chevelle at that point, so I figured it'd be a good way to test her."

"Okay," Amanda says. "I know I have a lot to learn, but I do want to watch."

If Amanda wants to learn, she can't begrudge her. Hopefully she's more dedicated to cars than she was her degree in, well, whatever she was going to school for before dropping out.

They may have met at university, but their friendship budded over the shared interest of fast cars.

"I didn't think it would be so weird seeing Ryder and Jordie again," Amanda says, huffing after her. She had almost forgotten that Amanda was there. Despite it being Amanda's garage, she had gotten lost in the moment.

Tuning Amanda's car has been somewhat of a distraction. Cars, unlike boys, are easy to handle and put together. It's for the best because if it weren't for this, she'd probably be tearing apart her Chevelle and likely doing more harm than good.

Amanda's trying to help but can only do so much, so she'd resolved to lounge against the shop counter and keep Natalie company. Another welcome distraction.

"Well, with what you told me about Jordie, I expected it to be awkward, but why with Ryder?" Natalie asks. To her memory, Amanda had never mentioned him before.

"It's just different. Been so long, I guess," she says, "And I was only really a tag-along before."

"Everybody is a tag-along until they get their own car," Natalie says. "You'll be fine."

Amanda nods, "I guess so."

The smell of motor oil is penetrating the relatively small garage, so she takes a break to lift the door, letting in the sweet summer air.

Amanda's chipping at her nail polish when Natalie walks back in, examining the car and deciding that she must wait for more parts before she can continue.

Amanda turns her gaze to the car. "That's it for today?"

Natalie nods and reaches for a beer that Amanda has taken out for her. "Yep. Whatever parts my supplier doesn't have, he'll get sent in."

"Awesome. So, when do you think it'll be ready?" Amanda asks.

"Optimistically, another week."

Amanda's face lights up, and Natalie smiles too, glad that this distraction from Ben is bringing joy to somebody considering her mind is rattling out of control.

"Do you want to come over? We could watch a movie or

something. Your place is kind of a disaster," she says, looking around at the filthy garage and thinking of the boxes upstairs that Amanda hasn't bothered to unpack. She didn't even see a TV in the small upper apartment.

"Not like I have other plans," Amanda says and jumps down, grabbing her purse. "We might as well."

Chapter 6: Jordie

He swallows his breath as he looks at the numbers he's written down. He's now $220,000 in debt to the mafa. He's lucky to be alive. Lucky, or are they biding their time?

"Are you okay?" Brooke asks, her voice softer than he's used to hearing.

Yeah. No. His entire world is ready to topple over. His debt keeps growing instead of decreasing. He may be winning sometimes, but the few times he does lose, it's not only his ass on the line. He's already dug himself in too deep, and he's not sure how he'll ever pay.

"Yeah, I am," he says. His stomach turns. He hates lying to his girlfriend.

If he tells Brooke that they're in serious danger of Jared coming after them, he may lose her too, and he can't afford that right now.

"Just tell me what's bothering you," she demands.

The less she knows, the better.

"I saw Amanda," he says, opting to shoot himself in the foot. Good enough excuse. He may not want to have this conversation, but it's a hell of a lot better than the real reason.

Brooke's face drains of all color. The room falls silent for what feels like six years.

"Where?" she asks after several more moments.

"At the last race," he says, drumming his fingers on the table. "She was talking to Ryder."

Brooke's nostrils flare.

"Did you talk to her?" she asks as if wanting to accuse Jordie of something.

"I didn't."

She nods and says, "Good."

Though he's not surprised, he can't help but think that Brooke is a little too insecure about Amanda, even going so far as obsessing over comparisons between them. Always asking too many questions about his relationship with Amanda.

He stands from the table and wraps his arms around her. "Brooke, you know I chose you, right?"

She nods, but her bottom lip quivers.

He places his finger on her lip, rubbing the edge gently. "I'll always choose you."

"Okay," she says. Her muscles relax, so he leans in and kisses her.

He tries to shake his own anxiety, but the number on the

piece of paper is haunting him. If he can't figure out a way to pay, he's not sure what he'll do.

Brooke leans back from him and pulls herself up to sit on the table, too close to the paper. He tightens but tries to force a smile. He has to keep this from her.

"I want to go to the next race with you," she says.

Brooke never goes to races. Brooke and Amanda together on the same strip of pavement could have devastating consequences. Saying no to his girlfriend could too.

He grits his teeth.

"Are you sure you want to go?" he asks.

Brooke crosses her arms and asks, "Why? Is there a reason I shouldn't go?"

He shakes his head. "No. But I don't even know if she's coming back, and you hate racing."

"I don't hate racing," she says. "I just don't like when girls like Amanda are there ogling you."

"It's not like that for me, and you know it."

She sighs audibly. "Yeah, I'm sure all of that female attention is absolutely horrible for you to deal with."

"Whatever. Come to the race if you want. Just be careful who you piss off."

"Piss off? Now I'm some vicious dog that needs to be kept on a leash?"

"You know that's not what I meant."

She jumps down from the table, placing her hands on his shoulders. "At this rate, I think the only danger is going to be one of us snapping and killing the other."

If only she knew the true danger that could very well be

facing them.

He places his hands on her waist, pecking her cheek with a quick kiss. "I could never hurt you."

"Yeah, not on purpose," she says.

Her face is more a smirk than a threat, but he nearly chokes. If anything does happen to her, it would be entirely his own fault. His selfish and stupid choices.

He pulls her closer, kissing her again, and then pulls away slightly to say, "You know I only love you, right?"

"I know. I just know that Amanda…"

"Is the past," he says.

"Okay," she says, her voice cracking as though she still isn't sure.

Chapter 7: Natalie

She turns the key and walks into her house. Most of the lights are dim, and the living room furniture is pretty dark considering the only lamp is in the corner by the television. It sits atop the white-brick fireplace that hasn't been lit in probably a decade.

Amanda's face turns to shock when she and Natalie walk into Natalie's place. Amanda clearly wasn't expecting Ryder to be sitting on the stark grey sofa. Natalie wasn't expecting it either, but only because he was supposed to be working.

"You're home early," she says, and he nods, putting down the car magazine he was rifling through.

"Yeah, there wasn't much left to do, so I took the rest of the night off," he sets down the television remote and looks at Amanda, head tilted.

Amanda doesn't seem to know what to do with herself. She and Ryder exchange glances.

"I didn't know you lived with Ryder," Amanda says, her cheeks flushed red.

"She has been for three years," he says, and he adds. "We're cousins. This was my father's house."

"Was?" Amanda asks, but covers her mouth with her hand after figuring it out for herself.

"Ryder's father passed away three years ago," Natalie says, then adds, "We're going to watch a movie. Do you want to join us?"

He holds his magazine in his hands, and his thumb looks ready to ball into a fist. "No," he says. "I think I'll take this to my room. Enjoy your night."

"Okay," she says.

Ryder doesn't look at Amanda again, just pushes past her and goes up the stairs to his room.

She turns to look at Amanda who just shrugs like she has no clue what that was about.

"So, you slept with my cousin," Natalie says when she's sure that Ryder is out of earshot.

Amanda's cheeks go red again, and she says, "No." She pauses, and then her eyebrow raises. "How did you know?"

"Kinda obvious," Natalie says. "Nobody reacts that way to an acquaintance."

Amanda flops herself onto the couch and sighs. "Yes, I did, but it was only one time. Years ago. And it was complicated."

"When isn't it complicated?" Natalie asks.

"Jordie had just cheated on me with Brooke and then left me. Ryder was… nice."

"A little too nice, apparently," Natalie says, and she tries not to think about it too hard because the thought of Ryder with anybody is gross.

"I liked him," Amanda says, and she sounds wistful as she talks about Ryder.

"Then what happened?" Natalie asks.

"I never went to another race until we went this week," she says. "I didn't want to see Jordie."

"You slept with him and then never saw him again?" Natalie asks.

"Not since the race," Amanda says, confirming, and she covers her face. "God, I suck. He must hate me."

Natalie sits next to Amanda, takes the remote, and turns on the television, searching through movies. "Nah, Ryder doesn't hate anybody. He's too busy for that."

"Then what about the cold shoulder?" Amanda asks.

"Ryder doesn't like anybody either; that was him being friendly." She's only half lying. Ryder pretty much has 3 friends to his name, and lately he's spent more time working or racing than he's spent with any of them.

Amanda covers her chest with one of the white couch cushions and settles in.

"Don't worry about Ryder," Natalie says.

Amanda nods and then suggests one of the movies on the screen.

Chapter 8: Axel

When he had accepted this job, he'd thought he would be making a difference. Catching criminals, making the world a better place. Instead, he's spent most of his time holed up in crappy motel rooms. His time's been spent following false leads and effectively chasing ghosts.

The best man for the job.

That's what his boss had said. Yeah, the best man for the job of sitting around and doing nothing.

Maybe he is the best man for the job. He's not been that great at his job lately. His track record is what? Letting people go and moping around.

Still, he's caught up here. Undercover. A shitty cover, too, cause he's pretty sure it's not going to take a lot of work for them to figure him out.

That's because this assignment is a punishment. They're

not concerned if he comes back alive. They're not going to say it officially, but he's disposable. Somebody else's problem. Catch the bad guys, or don't, just stay out in purgatory until you're useful again. Or dead.

Maybe it's time to turn in his badge and return home to Los Angeles. He can work with his father, or he can sleep on the streets. It'd be more comfortable than this motel.

Nope. He's not giving up just yet. Call it stubbornness, pride—anything but failure. He's looking through a file. Edge and Jared, two duelling brothers, have set up shop in different parts of the city.

Edge, formerly just Damien, is working for Prince, business tycoon who moonlights on the side. Of course, nothing could prove that Prince is involved. Prince is far too clean-cut and razor sharp for that. Prince may be taking home the profits, but Edge is the face of everything—dirty, gritty, and willing to get the job done.

Jared is just as formidable. However, he's unlikely to catch Jared with his tail between his legs. The better bet to getting in the door is through unpredictable Edge. The only common thread he could find on the surface was that the boys liked to fund street racers. Why? What about street racing had attracted not one, but two gangsters?

Maybe it was just a coincidence they both had drivers under their thumbs. Maybe. But that didn't sit well with him which is why he'd tracked down one of the drivers, Jordie Vodheo.

Jared and Edge needed drivers for something else. Something that required high speed and precision.

Jordie had gotten away, but he had at least found a lead.

That lead being enough kilos of cocaine to support the Upper East Side for a month and pay for a customized Mercedes.

For him, it was a win. For the boys upstairs, nope. 'Good for you', they chided. 'You have drugs and no drug dealers. This is one shipment out of hundreds per day. Good for you, idiot.'

Okay, they didn't call him an idiot out loud, but they did send him here to Chicago. To chase down fucking street racers and divulge their secrets. He's not even supposed to go after the big guys—just watch these kids play with their hot wheels.

Fun.

He half expected his next lead to be the corpse of Jordie hanging from an overpass or popping up in a river.

Instead, Jordie is very much alive, living his pathetic little life racing cars and pretending he's worth something.

The dude must have a guardian angel, 'else why's he still alive? Doesn't matter. What matters is that Jordie is the one person that can ID him, and he's part of the crowd he's supposed to be undercover with.

That's how little they care about his safety.

His only hope is to turn Jordie around, make him understand that whatever Jared has planned for him is going to be 100 times worse than ratting. As if. Right now, whatever's keeping Jordie alive is going to be nothing compared to the wrath he'd face if he talks.

Jordie hasn't said anything against him either because

he's still alive too.
Stalemate.

Chapter 9: Ben

"Still pining over that girl, kid?" Edge asks.

By now, Ben should be used to Edge's attempts at casual humour. Instead, he jolts in his seat at the question.

At 6'2, Edge isn't a small guy, but his personality is what makes him stand out. One minute he could be holding you against the wall, revolver to your throat, and the next he could be sipping lemonade and casually asking you what you think of his daughter. Ben always expected that it was a trap or a test, but whenever these kinds of questions came up, Edge always got irritable if you didn't answer.

"I don't know if it's really pining. I still think about her, I guess," he says. He doesn't want to be having this conversation. Dealing with Edge at times is like pulling teeth.

"I wouldn't know. I can't remember ever being in love with anyone. I mean, there was this girl that I thought I loved once, but when I considered stabbing her in the back to take over her business, I figured out that maybe it was just lust," he says and shrugs, pulling himself up onto his desk.

"I can see how that would end things," Ben says.

"Oh, it didn't end, we still see each other casually," Edge says. He's playing with a pencil and twirling it in his right hand. "She's awesome. Likes the colour red a little too much, but what can I say?"

"Must be some girl," Ben says and tries not to sound sarcastic. Edge makes it hard. The girl he's mentioning is in another mafia. He doesn't know her name, but he's heard a little about her. Her father was the head of a mafia, and for some reason, had bequest it to her.

The word *mafia* kind of trips him up. It feels weird. He spends a few seconds thinking about it—organization? Business? Whatever, mafia is good enough. It serves the purpose.

"So, have you even tried calling this broad, what's her name?" Edge asks, still playing with the pencil, and Ben tries not to get further distracted by his debate on terminology.

"Natalie," he says. "It won't change anything."

"You should just go to her house, break in, and then hide in her closet until she falls asleep. That way she won't be awake enough to complain when you talk to her," Edge says, the pencil falls to the floor, and Edge looks upset. "Damnit. Can you get me that pencil?"

Shaking his head, Ben picks up the pencil and hands it to the older, yet more childish, man. It's hard to believe that

Edge is considered one of the most feared members of the organization.

"I don't think I want to do that. I'll give her some space." Ben says, not sure if that's true.

"Whatever you think'll work, but don't come crying to me," Edge shrugs.

Ben doesn't mention that it was Edge who brought up the topic. It wouldn't have mattered to him, anyways. Besides, all Ben wants is to get out of there, and pressing the issue would just make the conversation last longer.

Edge's first name is Damien, but no one ever calls him that. Not even his relatives. Ben's pretty sure that Edge isn't even his real surname, especially since he has two brothers with the same parents and a different last name apiece. Apparently, if you're scary or crazy enough, you can just do anything, and people will go along with it.

Edge's office is antique in its setup. It has a large, brown, leather sofa, a bookshelf, and a large mahogany desk. If it wasn't for the crazy man kicking his feet into the desk, it would remind him of his father's. Too much so.

"I have your money," Ben says, his fingers drumming on his phone.

"Oh yeah, I forgot about that. You take this stuff way too seriously. Don't you ever have fun and stuff?" he says as he continues to kick his feet into the desk.

"Yes, I have loads of fun peddling drugs and smashing my car into buildings."

"Sounds like sarcasm. If I wasn't in such a good mood, I'd really be annoyed with you," Edge says before he takes a deep breath and opens his hands, expecting the money.

Ben brings the bills forward and places them in Edge's palms. They're calloused and show that his work has been anything but a full-time desk job.

"The rest will be here in a week."

"Yeah, yeah, I know the drill. When you come back, can you bring me a sub? I like subs." He's chewing on the end of the pencil.

"Are you serious?"

"Why on earth would I say something that I don't mean?" Edge questions, his eyes—just as gray as they are stone cold, stare into Ben's. "You'll bring it, right?"

"Uh, I guess so." He's perplexed. Why does Edge want him to bring a sandwich? It must be a test. Whatever.

The meeting finally ends. He goes to his car as quickly as he can, ready to go anywhere but there. Even home, with Ruth.

Chapter 10: Jordie

"One month," Jared says, "or else."

Or else what? Well, that's the part that he doesn't want to know. Or else he'll be in a body bag? Or cut into little pieces and fed to the fish in an extravagant manner?

Maybe he'll just be a few fingers fewer. Okay, he's pretty sure Brooke wouldn't be too happy if she had a boyfriend with anything fewer than 10 fingers and 10 toes.

Alive seems pretty important too.

"I want $20,000," Jared says. "That's not even a quarter. Consider yourself lucky."

Easy, right? $20,000 when he's so stressed, he can barely hold the clutch of his car without throwing up. He's going off the rails.

"Okay," he says. Can't exactly say no now, can he?

Jared nods at him. "Good, we're on the same page."

Yeah, same page. Sure.

"Don't be late," Jared says.

"I won't be," he assures Jared. Himself? Not so sure. Not so sure at all. Actually, he's the closest he's ever been to terrified.

Guess he could sell his car. Then what? Make less money? Be in the same situation the month after with no safety net?

He's fucked.

Chapter 11: Ben

Ben is greeted by the scent of cooked pasta when he walks into his apartment. Ruth is in front of the stove wearing only a small, black tank top and black underwear.

"That smells good," Ben says as he sits on the couch that's only about 6 feet away from the stove. He rests his head against the wall.

"I made it for you," she pours the pasta into a bowl and hands it to him. "I thought you might be hungry after work."

"Thanks. This is good." He takes a bite and smiles at her approvingly. He's usually not nice to Ruth even though she doesn't really deserve his anger.

Ruth sits next to Ben and rests her head on his shoulder. Her body is warm and soft. She's tiny but somehow not bony. If you didn't know that Ruth had an eating disorder, you might think she was just another skinny girl. You might even think she just hit the gym every day and that her life is perfectly normal.

She's not going to be there much longer, but at the moment, he wants to let her stay because he feels uncharacteristically lonely. Ruth probably belongs in therapy. That's none of his business.

Like clockwork, he thinks about Natalie.

Ben places the bowl, still half full, on the cheap plywood coffee table and wraps his arm around Ruth. Her head moves to his chest, and she yawns lightly. She's not much different in size than Natalie. Her scent is different, but if he closes his eyes, he can still pretend. "Ruth, you should probably eat something."

It's rare for Ben to get involved in Ruth's problems but feeling her tiny body against his frame is causing him some concern.

"I did eat. I had an apple," she says.

He isn't sure if Ruth is lying, but he can't force her to tell the truth.

"Okay. That's good."

Ruth reaches up and gently places a kiss on Ben's lips. For a few moments, he considers breaking away, but instead he returns the kiss, picking her up and pulling her atop of him.

Ruth kisses him. It can be hard to tell when she's actually happy because she always looks so sad.

She is cute—a little awkward, but cute. He pulls her waist closer to him and kisses her hungrily. The pasta was nothing compared to the sweet taste of her lips. He bites her bottom lip. He wants to lose himself in somebody—anybody, desperately.

He tries to push back the thought of Natalie as he and Ruth lock their hands and their bodies together. He can't get Natalie out of his head. He never can. He tries to hide his feelings in the kisses, but with every moment, he has to try harder. Ruth isn't ugly, and she isn't that annoying, but honestly, she isn't anything like Natalie. Ruth is nothing to him but a refuge, and it's not enough, but it's something.

He doesn't stop kissing her. They move positions, and he has her pressed against the back of the couch. Her hair is falling around her face, and her lips, naturally cherry red, are parted. He moves in for another kiss, her body pressing forward to meet his.

He can't stop, but it's not right. She will never be Natalie. He tries to stop comparing the two, but he can't. Natalie is headstrong, smart, and wouldn't give in as easily as Ruth has.

He stands, carrying Ruth in his arm; she's nearly weightless. It takes no effort to take her to the adjoining bedroom. He throws her on his bed. He looks at her with lust and nothing more, but it's okay because she does the same.

They'll both pretend they're with other people, he thinks as he crawls atop of her, ready to forget about Natalie, at least for a little while.

Chapter 12: Amanda

She has convinced herself that despite her past, she would be fine diving into the world of illegal street racing. Natalie had been working on her car for a week, and the anticipation was beginning to grow.

Some of her fear has dissipated. She might even be able to pull this off.

Except…

She stops dead in her tracks. He's three feet before her, close enough that she almost bumps into him. Every muscle in her body clenches. Despite every rational thought that's pushed him away, every year that's passed, he's standing in-front of her, next to his GTO, like nothing's changed; same leather jacket over a white shirt.

She lets out a breath as she tries to shake her brain and regain her composure.

"Amanda?" Jordie asks, eyes wide. Startled just as she is,

he blinks before saying, "Why are you here?"

Her heart rips in half for the millionth time since she's last seen him. Except, instead of a memory that fades into her thoughts just as she falls asleep or on cold nights where she's a little too lonely for her own good, he's here.

Why? She thinks. *Because you ruined my life*. You took away any normalcy I could have had, and you burned this world into my brain. You burned the adrenaline into my psyche. *I'm here because I have to be*, she thinks.

"It's a long story," she says.

She can hardly breathe.

It's like nothing has changed for a moment. She's tossed back to the 17-year-old girl that had fallen head over heels in love, who had spent late nights avoiding her parents, sitting in the passenger seat of Jordie's car. She doesn't know what she should say. *I miss you* is too much. What will he say after all this time?

Neither of them speaks.

Their relationship was never one for words. It was fast, passionate, fleeting…

Not sure what she should do, she reaches her arms out to hug Jordie. "How are you?" she asks.

He opens his arms and lets her hug him. Even pats her shoulder. His aftershave is so familiar, burned into her memory even after all these years.

It's not Jordie that answers.

"Amanda, nice to see you," Brooke says. Her voice grates like metal across asphalt.

Jordie quickly drops his arms from Amanda, and she

backs up two feet. Whatever flicker of emotion she had felt is replaced by ice.

Like he's some kind of prized possession Brooke hangs over him, inching closer and wrapping her arm around his waist, claiming him. Her first love. Brooke's forever love.

"Nice to see you too," she says, having to twist her face into something resembling a smile.

Brooke was that girl that no one talked to but also that girl who didn't make an effort to talk to you. Nearly invisible, Amanda wouldn't have cared about Brooke. As far as social hierarchy was concerned, Brooke didn't exist. She didn't matter. However, she became the girl who somehow got her hooks into Jordie, slept with him, and less than a week later, found a way to break him and Amanda up. She then became his new girlfriend.

Amanda stops herself from calling Brooke a bitch. At least out loud.

Chapter 13: Axel

His baseball cap rounds off the worst cover in the world. What's worse, while staking out Jordie's racing scene, he's come to realize that there's not one but two idiots who could rat him out.

From what he can tell, most of the racers are kids. From late teens to mid-twenties, they're playing street racers and dabbling in small-time drug dealing to feel like they're somebody.

Not only are they children, they're not even intelligent children. Take for instance Jordie; the kid can't be more than 24, and he's embedded with a ruthless criminal.

Axel's file on Jared confirms over a dozen deaths. Those were the blatant hits. There were many others—faceless people—who the law would never find and cases that looked accidental enough that no one could ever prosecute.

Yet here they are. Kids playing in their modified cars as

though driving an illegal vehicle makes you something other than a fucking idiot.

He wonders if these children would still feel so delighted by their rebellion if they had seen the mangled corpses of their brethren that littered the morgues.

They're so stupid, they'd probably still do it anyways.

It's not like he doesn't enjoy fun himself. Everybody speeds their car sometimes or steps over the edge.

However, not everybody is so desperate for thrill-seeking that they actively ignore sanity.

Maybe his profession is another sense of thrill-seeking, one marred by entitlement. The crushing weight of thinking that you're meant to protect others when really all you're doing is circling a merry-go-round, catching criminals that later get out only to find another just like them.

Crime never stops.

Never sleeps.

Catch one, another comes in their place.

Chapter 14: Natalie

She stands with her back against the wall, Ben facing her. They're between two buildings, away from prying eyes and ears. His eyes are colder than they used to be. His hands more worn down too.

"Nat," he says, leaning into her. "I want you back."

She shakes her head. "No, you don't."

He leans close enough that she can feel his hot breath on the nape of her neck. Her legs quiver.

"I already told you, no."

His hand lands on her waist, already sensitive, her back arches against the building.

"Ben," she says, her voice drawling. "We can't do this, not again."

His eyes, ocean blue tonight, tempt her further, filled with lust and maybe something softer—but only flickering for a second. Desperation, or some other bullshit.

She'd take the lust, but the rest of it…

"I want this," he says, lifting her hand to his mouth and biting the top of her thumb. He pulls her hand back to the tip of his lips, whispering, "I need this."

She needs this to end. But the attraction doesn't just disappear.

He was supposed to be the stupid college boyfriend, the type of person you date while you're still getting your bearings.

The guy that hangs out at frat parties and ends up happily married to some blonde lady named Alice or Susan.

"Nat?" Ben asks, almost whines.

Yeah, she's gotten a bit distracted.

"You don't need me," she says, still wondering how they had gotten so off track in their lives. "You're just unhappy with how your life is going."

He shakes his head, one hand still firmly on her waist, massaging the skin where her tank top had flipped up to expose flesh.

She should be resisting.

But his lips taste so damn good when he leans in to kiss her, letting his tongue linger and flicking her teeth.

Her own arms move to his back, grabbing him so that she can get closer, letting him taste her.

It doesn't take long for him to push her firmly against the wall, using his strong hands to hoist her up to his waist, wrapping her legs around him.

The humming of cars in the distance, the chattering, and the screeching of tires isn't enough to stop her.

Chapter 15: Axel

2 Months Ago

Axel sits in the office of the Chicago branch. He's usually stationed out of Florida, monitoring shipments that go back and forth to Latin America. Now, he's sitting in the director's office, and Axel knows this isn't going to be good. At Quantico, he was one of the top students—always on the ball and able to get the job done. It turns out, reality is more complicated than simulations and exercises.

"Agent Wariloe," the director says, his brow furrowed. "It's come to my attention that we have a situation with your most recent case."

"Yes sir," Axel says, full-well knowing that there's nothing else he can say.

Axel feels like a child with his hand stuck in the cookie jar.

"So, Agent Wariloe, can you explain to me how you lost the driver but somehow got his car?"

"He must have been spooked," Axel says. "I looked for him, but he wasn't there."

"You looked for him, but he wasn't there?" the director asks, tapping his fingers on the desk.

"Yes sir," Axel says again.

"So, I'm supposed to believe that this twenty-something year old street-racer outsmarted one of my best agents?"

"I guess so," Axel says, his hands in his lap.

He wonders if this is going to be his last time in the office. This might be the end of his career as an agent.

The director writes something down on a piece of paper—notes of Axel's failure that will probably reside in some file for the rest of his career and longer.

"Either you're grossly incompetent, or you're corrupt enough that you let him go," the director says. "At least that's how this looks, Wariloe."

"I know," Axel says. "It was a mistake."

"I believe you," the director says. He taps his pen. "That doesn't mean others will. You're staying in Chicago; I want you to keep close eyes on the street racers, figure out who the players are and what's going on with Jared and Edge."

"You want me to stay in Chicago?" Axel asks in disbelief.

"Somebody needs to be our eyes on the ground," the director says.

Axel knows that it's really a way of saying, "We're keeping our eyes on you."

"Okay," Axel says. "Thank you, sir."

They stand, and he shakes his hand, but the director's eyes are sullen. The trust is broken—and it might never be fixed.

Chapter 16: Jordie

Fuck.

Yeah, he knew this was going to happen. Maybe not the stupid hug, like, why'd he fucking do that? Anyways, the point is, he knew this was going to happen. Hell, it's what Brooke wanted. A showdown. Who needs cars when two women that completely hate each other could just claw the eyes out of the other? Great.

Back to the hug. Why didn't he push her away? He could have easily done so. It's not like a 5'2 girl who weighs a total of 110 lbs could actually put up a fight. Why? Well, because he misses her. Just because they broke up doesn't mean that every childhood memory had evaporated too.

What's the rule book for cheating on your childhood friend turned girlfriend with the woman you completely fell in love with? He figures it's something other than hugging the first girl at a race where you totally know your girlfriend is nearby.

Yeah, well. He's stupid. These girls make him stupid. Always have, clearly.

"I was just asking Amanda what she's doing here," he says. A little too defensively. Dial it back, he thinks. Yeah, be cool. Totally cool.

He wraps his arms around Brooke too. See, they're a completely happy couple with absolutely no problems. Nobody is jealous, nobody has pent-up resentment. Everybody is fine. While he's at it, the mafia isn't totally pissed at him either.

Brooke tightens her own hand on his waist. Any tighter and her nails are going to draw blood.

He watches Brooke as she watches Amanda, ready for the fight. "So, what are you doing here, Amanda? I'm sure it's a great story," Brooke says.

Yeah, great story. Something completely unrelated to him. Right? Please fucking be right.

"I just felt an intense desire to skip town after the end of a relationship," Amanda says.

They're all still fake smiling. Better a façade than a war.

"Who were you dating?" is all Jordie asks. Should he have asked? Brooke's grip tightens, her nail digging slightly. Yeah, nope.

"Scott Dubrea," Amanda says; her nose scrunches. She licks her lips.

He's sure Brooke would be pissed if she knew that inside his mind, he still knows the tells for when Amanda is uncomfortable. Then again, who isn't uncomfortable in this conversation?

"Never heard of him," he shrugs.

"Me neither. Where does he work?" Brooke asks. Casual talk about the other man. Brooke is dwelling on Amanda moving on. Fair play, Brooke.

"He was a club manager at Echo," Amanda says, shifting her feet.

Brooke loosens her grip on him. Her eyes leer at Amanda,

"So, Amanda, that doesn't really answer the question. Why are you here?" Jordie asks, a little too curious considering Brooke's scowl, but he wants to know.

"I'm here for the same reason you are. To race."

He's half-relieved that he's not the reason but the other half is bewildered.

"You're here to race?" Jordie scoffs. "God, you are stupid."

Brooke doesn't say anything.

"Why?" Amanda asks, her eyes wide. "I expected you to laugh at me but to call me stupid? You've been racing for years."

"This shit isn't for everybody," he says. He pauses for a moment, his face tightening. "It's poison."

"It's what I want to do," she says, "I've got to find Natalie. Have a nice night."

She nods at Brooke who nods back.

Cordial enough, he thinks, but he finds out that he was totally wrong three seconds later, right after Amanda's out of earshot.

"What the fuck was that?" Brooke demands.

"I don't know, two old friends catching up?"

"Why was she hugging you like she was ready to slip into your pants?"

"She wasn't. It was just a hug. I hug lots of my friends."

Brooke crosses her arms. "No, you don't."

"Okay, I don't, but I do when I haven't seen them in years."

"And you haven't, right?" Brooke huffs.

"Uh. Yeah?"

"Fine, but you just warned her off street racing like you care about her well-being. Seriously. What the fuck?"

His temple bulges. "I thought you wanted her gone?" he asks.

"I want her gone, not you involved in her business."

His eyes roll, "Brooke, this was nothing. Why are you acting so jealous?"

Rule #1: Absolutely never accuse your girlfriend of being jealous. Even if she is.

"Don't put this off on me," she says, pacing around the side of the car. "It's not like you don't have a history of cheating on people."

"I cheated with you," he pleads.

"Yeah, on her. So, morally speaking, if you went back to her, it wouldn't even register ethically."

"That's not how that works…" he says.

"Jordie…" her voice drawls out.

"Yeah?" he asks.

She sighs and shakes her head, "I'm sorry."

He shrugs like none of this is even happening, distracted and staring off in the other direction.

"So, we're good?"

He nods, eyes focused elsewhere. "Yep, we're good, but I'm going to race now."

"Okay," she says, but he's already walking away.

Chapter 17: Axel

He watches as Jordie interacts with two girls: one is a blonde, and the other is an unhinged brunette that he recognizes from his file aSs Brooke.

Not only is the kid a pain in the ass, he's managed to drive the female population crazy too. Great. Just more people to potentially get involved in this already messy situation.

After the girls are finally done with their CW-worthy conversation, Jordie's eyes catch his. He nods at him.

Axel waits for him to come over, free of the girls.

When Jordie approaches, Axel rolls his eyes. "Girl problems?" Axel asks.

Jordie shrugs. "It's nothing."

"Good, because I don't really care," he says. "So, you're still in the racing game even after you lost your last car chase?"

Jordie stares back at him, almost dumbfounded.

How dare Axel have the nerve to bring up the time that he came out of a drug bust sans driver and Jordie sans car?

"For now," Jordie says. "But I won't be if anybody figures out who you are. What are you doing here?"

"You know why I'm here," Axel says.

Jordie's voice is lower as he watches Axel, saying, "You already screwed me with the car and drugs. My ass is on the line."

"And whose fault is that?" Axel asks. He's not about to feel sorry for Jordie for his own actions.

"I'm not helping you," Jordie replies.

"What about her?" Axel asks, pointing to Brooke, who seems to be amusing herself by typing something into her cellphone, clearly the least interested in racing there.

"You're not going to do anything to her," Jordie says, so sure of himself he's almost smirking. "You have ethics, remember?"

Axel nods. "I do have ethics, that's true."

Jordie crosses his arms on his chest, proud of himself.

"That's the thing with ethics, though. They don't apply to murderers," Axel says, trying his best to hide his own smile. Nobody likes the smug guy.

Jordie, now serious, is watching Axel closely. "What murderer?" he asks, his bodyweight shifting.

"Cut the crap, Jordie," he says. "The point is, I have a hunch about your girlfriend's absentee father, and I'd love to find his body so that she can finally find closure."

He watches as Jordie tries to manage his breath, playing

the cool guy. He's trying not to squirm so much.

"We've moved on from that," he says. "Her father is part of the past."

Axel nods and says, "Then I guess it would be great if it were kept under wraps."

"I can't help you," he says. "If I do, that's the end of me. I'm not even sure why I'm still here. Besides, I can't even be trusted with any info."

Axel pulls his baseball cap down closer over his eyes, adjusting it and hoping that nobody is paying much attention to their conversation or his face.

"You're probably right," he says, but when he thinks about it, they're both screwed either way. "But I need something."

Chapter 18: Brooke

She approaches Amanda alone. Jordie's gone off to race, so it's the perfect time to corner the blonde who intimidated her for years.

"You need to stay away from Jordie," Brooke says, her teeth showing as she talks.

"Excuse me?" Amanda asks, acting like she doesn't know why Brooke is acting this way.

"Oh, come on, Amanda. You suddenly show back up after years, and you expect me to believe that it has nothing to do with Jordie? You're not exactly Mario Andretti," Brooke says, her blood boiling at the thought of Amanda prancing around trying to take Jordie back from her as though this war wasn't already won.

"I don't know what you're talking about," Amanda says, rolling her eyes dismissively. "Not everything is about Jordie. Actually… nothing is."

"I don't believe you," Brooke says, almost spitting on Amanda.

She's ready to claw her eyes out. If they were lions, she would already be pouncing, but since they're not, and this is a public place, she settles by saying, "Stay away or else."

"Or else what?" Amanda asks.

"I don't know," Brooke says, and she really doesn't. All she knows is that she wants Amanda to leave.

Amanda shakes her head and then says, "I don't want your boyfriend," before she turns around and walks away.

It's not like Brooke can follow her without making a scene.

She shouldn't be insecure about Jordie talking to Amanda. She hasn't even seen her in 4 years, and she was the one who stole Jordie from Amanda. Except she's still intimidated by her. Not that she's going to admit that to Jordie.

Back in high school, Amanda was the "It Girl". The Serena Van Der Woodsen of the halls. Everybody loved Amanda, and very few people paid attention to Brooke. Not that she wanted to be paid attention to, but complete invisibility wasn't much fun either.

Between her home and school life, Brooke was pretty depressed for a lot of her teen years. How could she not be? The fact Jordie Vodheo, the king of the school, had wanted anything to do with her even as friends was a bit of a shock.

Seeing Amanda reminds her of the girl she was in high school again—meek, sad, and still under the thumb of Aaron. It also reminds her of a time where she felt suffocated by sadness and a lack of willpower.

Jordie knows how much she dislikes Amanda. She definitely shouldn't be throwing threats around either, but whatever.

The problem is that Jordie has always had street racing, friends, and even fans. People who wanted to be around him. For Brooke, all she has is Jordie.

The codependence isn't healthy, and it's certainly not a great life-plan, but all she wants is to be with Jordie. Together, somewhere, in their own little home. She doesn't need much else.

Chapter 19: Jordie

Jordie never intended to get involved with Jared. He was content street racing for fun here and there. He didn't need to run drugs or amass more and more debt. But Jared knew he could use Jordie's driving skills, and Jared knew where the body was buried. Literally.

Jordie's now caught on that Jared is smarter than Jordie. When Jordie first started out, Jared made him think he wanted Jodie to be there.

Made him think he was somebody, or could be at least.

It was easy and fast money.

But he's learned that it's never easy, even when it's fast.

Eventually, he had to keep going just to keep up. He needed to ensure that his racing skills, and his driving, stayed well in the range of what Jared could use. He had to stay useful, be somebody that could be relied upon.

Until he wasn't.

Nobody's perfect, right?

He puts his head in his hands. He's fucked up one too many times.

That doesn't mean that he needs to listen to Axel hounding him day and night, pretty much stalking him. The dude is what, 35? Doesn't he have something better to do than to read him the riot act over and over?

He thinks on his feet quickly, surveying the crowd and seeing others that he knows.

"Let's race," he proclaims, loud enough that passersbys can hear his challenge.

Axel shakes his head in protest, his stupid cap still pulled down over his eyes as he says, "No."

Jordie smirks; he may not be able to control what Axel knows, but he's not going to let him ruin the night—especially not after throwing threats around.

"Come on, buddy, you're going to talk shit, we'll race," Jordie says, leaning in closer to Axel and speaking in a lower voice, "If you're going to spend your day following a street racer, maybe you should plan to fit in."

Axel crosses his arms. "I don't have a car."

"What about that perfectly good one I left you with?" Jordie says. Probably not the best to brag about it, but his blood is still boiling from the threat toward Brooke.

"Junk heap considering you outran the car," Axel says, arms still crossed. "I'm not going to race you. Grow up."

"You tracked me down at a race, and I want to race," he says, teeth clenched. "So, let's race."

Axel groans before saying, "Still don't have a car."

Jordie shouts, "Come here," in the direction of Andy, the first driver he sees that he at least knows. They may be on different pillars of the drug world, but he figures Andy can easily be swayed.

Andy turns his head, watches them, and walks over. He's smirking.

"Yeah?" he says, his eyes on Axel.

"I want you to meet my friend, Axel," Jordie says, patting Axel's shoulder.

Andy's right eyebrow lifts, his expression quizzical. "Your friend?" he asks.

"Yeah, Axel has an affinity for car chases, but sadly he doesn't have a car," Jordie says, using his finger to flip Axel's hat off his head. "Can he borrow yours?"

Axel watches the hat fall, grimaces, picks it up, but doesn't put it back on his head.

Andy's eyes move up and down, watching Axel, then he turns his head to his EVO. "Have you raced before?" he asks.

Axel shakes his head. "No, I haven't."

Andy laughs, lost somewhere in his own little world. As far as Jordie can tell, Andy's always been a little off.

Andy hands Axel the keys a little too quickly.

Jordie slaps Axel's shoulder once more. "Great, so now you have a car."

Disdain flashes across Axel's face. Jordie's never seen a man unhappier with his surroundings. Good. Whatever Axel knows about Brooke, and whatever shitstorm awaits him on the other side.

"Fine," Axel says, then he nods at Andy and says, "Thank you."

Jordie walks toward The Judge. Even if his opponent is Axel, he's still pretty enthused about racing. Hell, he's more excited because he's been living this moment in his head for months. Thinking about what it would be like to out-run Axel, car intact, a complete do-over of all of his problems.

The change in Axel's demeanor, that of a man with a strong grudge, shoulders raised, tells Jordie that Axel has been thinking the same. Axel may not be a racer, and he might not want to do this, but he's reasonably sure that Axel relives that night too.

The night he lost the car and the drugs replays in his head over and over. Sure, he didn't get arrested, but that was the night things turned extra shitty for him. Axel is pretty much the human embodiment of everything wrong in Jordie's life.

Jordie gets behind the wheel of The Judge as Axel, grimacing the entire time, gets into Andy's crappy Mitsubishi. As far as Jordie's concerned, this race is a done deal. It might not solve everything, but at least it'll feel good at the time.

Behind the wheel is one place that Jordie can find some semblance of control. He starts his car and moves it toward the start-finish line drawn with chalk on the blocked off back-road. Axel does the same.

One of the guys at the race holds up a flag to signify the race is about to begin. Jordie revs the engine of his car, letting it roar for everybody in the crowd to hear. He turns to look at Axel in the car beside him while grinning his brightest grin and trying to push the anxiety of his situation deep below the surface.

The flag drops, and Jordie presses down on the gas, letting the car go as fast as she wants to, passing the Mitsubishi, and spiraling toward the first turn of the race. Nothing helps Jordie when he's miserable more than racing. That is, nothing helps him more than the feeling of being first.

He continues to lead for 90 seconds, an eternity when you're behind the wheel going 200mph, but Axel is somehow right behind him now—inching closer and closer as they turn once more, almost catching him by going wide on the outside.

Jordie manages to maintain his speed for another half mile, but Axel is still there behind him as they come back toward the start/finish line. Jordie can feel his blood start to boil. This was supposed to be his time to shine, to prove to Axel that he's better than him.

Except now Axel is pushing past him with 20 feet to go. He watches in disbelief as the Mitsubishi passes The Judge and appears to fly past the finish line, driving in a careful and calculated victory circle around a group watching the race. As Jordie drives past the finish line himself, he doesn't stop driving.

From his rear-view mirror, he can see Axel step out of the Mitsubishi and simply nod his head toward Jordie who keeps driving, making a left-hand turn toward an area he doesn't even know.

Chapter 20: Natalie

"Is there any hope for us?" Ben asks her outright.

"No," she says. "There's not."

His steel-blue eyes widen. She half expects them to flicker black like a demon in a teen drama.

He holds his hands up to his head, his fingers entangling his short brown hair.

"Why do you have to say that?" he asks.

"Because it's true," she sighs. "I've told you again and again."

"You ruined my life too, remember?" he snaps.

He goes cold. Old Ben has been replaced swiftly with Angry Ben. The guy she hates. The guy that snaps every time he's pissed off—hell, snaps in general because he's always pissed off. Tumultuous, even.

"You played a rather large part in that, I recall," she says, then sighs. It's not the first time he's tried to rope her back into his grasp. Using an emotional connection against her.

Maybe he shouldn't have lost his scholarship—pissed it all away because his feelings were hurt.

Maybe he shouldn't have kept driving.

He probably shouldn't have kept lying.

And it's not like it was a great idea to start drinking and cutting classes. To go from a 3.6 to a 2.5 GPA.

"Do you remember the night you broke up with me?" Ben asks.

"Of course I do," she says. "Why do you ask?"

"I don't know, I've thought of it a lot lately."

"I should go find Amanda," she says. Which is totally true because Amanda is here somewhere waiting for her.

Ben's eyes roll so hard, she thinks he might get an aneurysm. His darkness has been temporarily replaced with irritation.

"Why are you even hanging around with the princess?" he asks, his grimace saying more than enough without his snarky comment.

"We're *friends*," she says. "Something you might understand if you had any."

Ben closes the small gap between them. Angry Ben isn't grimacing, he's pretty much snarling.

"You and I are still friends," he says. His eyes never leave her, not even to blink. "And this isn't over."

She pushes his chest with her right hand, just enough to give her a foot between them. "I'm going now."

He doesn't speak as she starts to edges past him.

Ryder approaches them, head tilted slightly like he's

considering asking her about the exchange, but instead he asks, "Are you guys going to race?"

Natalie nods her head and watches Ben tense up. The two had never gotten along, and despite Ryder saying nothing about the relationship, she's pretty sure Ryder would rather she be with anybody else on earth.

Ben barely acknowledges Ryder and turns to kiss Natalie's cheek, watching just slightly from the corner of his eye to see how Ryder reacts. Ryder doesn't react outwardly; he just swings his car keys and motions to his Supra and says, "I'll be in my car," and leaves the two of them to finish up their torturous conversation.

"You didn't have to show off," she says. "You know he doesn't like you."

Ben laughs and then shrugs. "He just doesn't know how awesome I am, but I could show him if you ever let me come over and hang out at your house."

That's what she needs, Ben and Ryder in the same room watching bad action movies and commenting on just how terrible her cooking is. She imagines a night of burnt mac n' cheese and action flicks. She cringes visibly.

"What?" Ben asks, his hands on her waist. "I want to see you more."

"That's not a good idea," she says, shaking her head. "Besides, I never hang out at home. I just go there to eat and sleep and then spend most of the day out and about."

"Yeah, working your shit job," he says. "Couldn't you get something else with your degree?"

"Who says I wanted something else with my degree?"

"You're content working part-time in a used clothing store?" he asks, trying to hide the judgement from his voice but failing miserably.

"That's a bit snobbish for a drug-dealer, don't you think?" she says, "Besides, it's vintage."

"This is temporary, I'm not going to do it forever. It's just until I can pay for law school."

She raises her eyebrow. "So, you're going to break the law… to become a lawyer? Isn't that shooting yourself in the foot before you even walk over the threshold?"

"Criminals need lawyers more than anybody. It's job security."

She shakes her head and suppresses a laugh before she says, "Right. Time to race."

But Ben isn't having it and takes her hand, squeezing it.

 "Seriously, Nat, you're brilliant with vehicles, with any machine. Why aren't you looking for a job in engineering?" he asks.

"Because I don't want to do that anymore," she says, and pulls her hand back.

"Why?" he asks.

"I just don't want to do it. It wasn't a good fit."

"That's bullshit," he says. "I've seen you with the cars, it's like you're completely in awe of how things work. You should be doing something with that."

She shrugs and then turns to walk toward her car.

"Natalie, don't walk away from me," he says, but she doesn't listen.

He's probably shaking his head behind her, but she

doesn't want to deal with it. Yeah, she should go into engineering, and he should stop being a drug-dealer, but it doesn't look like either of them are going to change any time soon.

Chapter 21: Ben

Ben does three things when he gets home. The first is to put his money in a canister on the counter, the second is to change into a pair of PJ pants, and the third is to talk to Ruth and kick her out. He does each of these with the same weight of importance because none of them really matters to him.

As sad as it is to think about, he doesn't care about Ruth's feelings. He needs to be alone, and she needs to get lost. They weren't even dating, so it wasn't hard to do. A simple "get out" sufficed.

Where did Ruth go? He's not sure. Home, back to rehab. Maybe she hopped a plane to Japan. Not his fucking problem.

He would rather be alone forever than try to drown the memory of Natalie away.

He sits at his table, rolled up piece of paper in hand.

White lines spread across the dirty surface.

He questions, for a second, if the dirt has any danger, then he laughs at the irony. Yes, the dust will hurt him, not the cocaine.

He shakes his head. He's not sure who he does it for; he's alone in the apartment.

He leans toward the substance, scrunching his nose and moving along the line, seizing the powder, letting it shoot up inside him.

He thinks of the candy straws with powder he used to enjoy as a child.

Better than candy, he thinks.

No drug is enough to make him forget her. Nothing will ever make him forget. Her shadow lingers in the corner of the room, more like the ghost of a memory. Her smile, her lips.

His own failure consuming him.

He kicks a pile of books on the floor and watches them scatter. He hasn't had time to read them, but sometimes he likes to remember who he used to be.

He was never supposed to be a drug-runner. Just a few runs here and there, but what he's learned about Edge is this: it doesn't matter what you signed up for. You do what Edge says, or else…

Or else what? That's a question he doesn't want answered.

The shipments are easy enough. Drive to the drop spot. Pick up the drugs, and then drive them to the dealers. Easy enough. Don't get caught. Don't make stops. Again, don't get caught.

From what he can tell, Edge and Jared are rushing to expand their drug empires across the entire East Coast. He doesn't have details, but the runs are getting longer and longer. It used to all be within state, but now they have him breaking federal laws, crossing borders with illegal substances. He's fine driving and dropping off so long as the cash keeps coming in.

Chapter 22: Amanda

She inhales. Diving headfirst means that there is no room for regret, for past feelings. She wants to race, and she wants to be good. She's spent enough of her life around racers to know that nobody is born great or even born good enough. It takes time, practice, and expertise. The best racer she knows is never going to help her with her problems. So, she's going to have to go to the second.

"Ryder," she says as she walks up to him, taking a quick deep breath and then blurting out, "I have a favor to ask you."

He's sitting in his car, door open, stereo blaring. He toys with the dial, changing the song. "Seriously?" he says then scoffs, shaking his head before continuing. "After all these years, you think you deserve a favour?"

"Well, I just wondered if…" she says as she watches him closely, trying to surmise if he hates her or just thinks she's a pathetic mess. "Will you help me get used to my car?"

Ryder looks at Amanda and shakes his head, then says, "I don't have time to waste on somebody who will just take off again."

Amanda bites her lip. "I—," she starts.

Ryder interrupts her, shaking his head as he speaks, "Save it."

"I guess I didn't realize you cared so much."

"I didn't care," his eyes go dark, and he exhales. "We had meaningless sex in the Supra, and then I didn't see you for four years. Still not sure why I should help you."

Ouch. She nods, biting her lip again. What more could she say? Yep. She definitely left. Didn't come back either. Instead, she enrolled in college, shacked up with a bartender, and eventually dropped out of college.

"I guess I don't," she says, her voice soft. "I just can't think of another driver as good as you. I'm asking you for help because I think you're the best."

Well, *second best*, she thinks again. Still, Ryder is unlikely to help her unless he knows that she's out of options. Her pride aside, Ryder is her best hope to drive and not fall flat on her face.

"The best?" he asks, rolling his eyes. "Stop trying to flatter me."

"I'm telling the truth," she says.

He nods, then says, "I know you're telling the truth. But that doesn't mean you're not trying to flatter me."

He stands from the car, stretching his arms. She can see the hint of his muscles from underneath his green shirt, the same color as his car and his eyes.

"I thought Natalie was helping you with your attempt to give your father a heart attack," he says, closing the distance between them and leaning against his car.

"She *is,* but we both know that she's the one with talent under the hood. You're the one who excels behind the wheel," she says.

Natalie is a good driver, but Ryder could have been a pro if he wanted.

He nods. "Fair point. Still, why now?" he asks.

She's not sure how to answer the question. Perhaps it's because her college career is officially over, or because she's just gotten out of another relationship, or maybe she's just run out of excuses to ignore her fear.

"Why not now?"

"It was just a question," he says.

"I want to race. Isn't that enough?"

"Sure," he says. "But you're going to need more than sheer will to win."

He pauses for a few moments then continues.

"I'll help you," he says, and then crosses his arms. "But try not to make me regret it."

"What about tomorrow morning; could you meet me in my garage?" she asks. The thought of Ryder in her grimy garage is a little unnerving, but it's just another sacrifice she'll have to make if she's going to actually race. "Yeah. I'll meet you in the morning," he says.

Chapter 23: Natalie

An open envelope she had tossed aside sits on the coffee table. She takes a shot of vodka, despite it being 9am, and tries to forget that it ever came. Her hair is still a mess, and she's still in the PJ pants and silk tank top from the night before. It should be law that mail can only ruin your day after lunch.

It's not that the letter is exactly bad, but she doesn't want to deal with it. Or anything, really.

Ryder enters the living room, not yet shaved, and his expression turns quizzical. "Vodka?" he asks.

She nods.

"What's wrong?" he asks, rubbing his eyes.

"Nothing," she says.

Ryder nods, and turns to go to the kitchen. "Okay then," he says.

She takes the envelope back in her hands and removes

the piece of paper. *Last chance to apply to our Mechanical Engineering Master's Program* is written at the top in perfectly spaced Times New Roman.

What was once her dream, in fact all she wanted, seems like a life sentence. She rips the paper into 6 pieces, letting the words turn into nothing more than blotches of ink on separated pieces of paper, and throws them like confetti to the floor. She uncaps the vodka and pours another shot, slicking it back.

She can't imagine herself in a classroom, on a work program trying to put the pieces together, or designing machinery. In fact, she's not sure that her degree was worth the time she spent on it. The little use it gets is ensuring that the Chevelle remains street ready.

She's not sure of the exact moment that she decided to give up on whatever future she was supposed to have. At least, not the exact day that her plans had changed from ambition to uncaring and then eventually to the disdain she now feels. She's not even sure that she's given up on the dream completely—but for now, there's no way in hell she can go back to school. It's not easy to try and fix things when she's not even sure what's broken inside of her.

Ryder comes back in the living room holding two cups of coffees. He hands her one, and she accepts it, taking a sip and washing away the bitter remains of the vodka.

"Gonna tell me what that is?" he asks, pointing at the papers.

"Just a last chance memo for grad school admissions," she says.

"Ah," he replies, setting his coffee down next to the vodka. "Not going back?"

"Nope," she says.

Ryder falls silent for a moment before speaking. "I think you'd make one hell of an engineer," he says, "but if you don't want to, oh well."

"Oh well?" she asks, expecting him to judge her or try and force her to go. When she had told her mother that she wasn't going to apply, she had completely flipped out, even insisting that she was breaking her heart.

"It's just school," he says. "You'll figure it all out."

She takes another sip of the coffee and nods at Ryder, glad that he's not being too judgemental.

"I have to get ready for work," he says, standing up and taking his coffee with him. "You going to be okay?" he asks.

She nods, and she's not actually sure she won't be okay. Maybe she will be. She takes another drink of coffee instead of the vodka. That has to be a step forward, right?

Chapter 24: Brooke

If Jordie had trusted her enough to actually speak to her, she would have warned him not to sell his soul to the devil.

He had told her he had everything under control. He had insisted that everything was fine. His debt was going down. They would buy a small house. Everything was going to be different.

Then the devil himself called upon her.

"Brooke, it's been a while," he says. He's wearing a white t-shirt and jeans. He looks so harmless.

"You called me about Jordie," she says, her voice shaking. "What exactly is this about?"

Jared sits at his desk and folds his hands. "You know, Jordie has earned me a lot of money, but lately he's been losing—and he's not been paying. We've also had investors lose money against him."

"How much does he owe?" she asks.

"Right now? Or in general?" Jared unfolds his hands and places them on the desk. A crooked smile flits across his face right before he speaks again. "I don't think you'll like either answer."

"Both," she says. Jordie may be too fragile to tell her, but she needs to know. If she's going to clean up his mess, she's going to have to know the stakes.

"$22,000 right now and $220,000 in general," he says coolly.

"Okay," she says. Her mind swirls. Maybe not a lot of money in the grand scheme of things, but it's enough for a down payment on that house Jordie promised her.

She's not getting her fucking house, is she?

Figures.

The air she breathes through her nostrils stings. What's she supposed to do with this information?

"Why did you call me here?" she asks.

"Because there was a time when we were friends, Brooke." Hah. Friends. Good one, Mr. Mafia. "I helped you," he says,

"So, now I owe you, not the other way around. Why did you call?"

"That's precisely why. You owe me," he says. He taps his pen on his desk, his tongue grazing the back of his front teeth.

"I'm not following your logic here."

"Well, it occurred to me that the best way to hurt Jordie would be to hurt you. I don't want to hurt you, though," he says and lets the pen drop.

"Thank god for small favours, I guess," she says and crosses her arms.

"I can't let the money go, so what do you suggest I do about Jordie?"

She uses her hand to pull the hair on her left side out of her face. "How did it get this far? He hasn't been losing that much."

"Interest. Car parts. Lost bets. Every cent adds up. The point is he owes me money, and I don't know what to do about it," he says, and he stands from his desk. "So, what should I do?"

Brooke bites her lip. There's no way that this has all come up because Jordie's been losing; not entirely. She can always tell his mood after a race. "What aren't you telling me?"

Jared eyes her as though he's debating whether she can handle what he's about to say. "What I told you was true; it just wasn't the entire story," he says.

"What do you mean?" she asks.

"Jordie wanted to get out of debt, so I offered him a few jobs. Nothing too hard, just moving some drugs. About two weeks ago, he came back, but the car and its contents didn't."

"What happened to them?"

"According to Jordie, he was pinned down. They got the car, but miraculously, not him."

What the hell?

"And apparently, he didn't mention anything to you about it," Jared says, folding his arms across his chest.

"Apparently," she says.

"So, the question is, how did the cops get the car, and how did Jordie get off scot free?"

"That does seem like a pretty interesting question," she says. "But more importantly, what are you going to do about it?"

She's pissed off at Jordie, but she doesn't want him dead.

"Brooke, I think what happened with your father proves I don't want to hurt you, but I can't just let this slide. I have a reputation to uphold and a business to run."

She nods in understanding. "Well, let me work for you. I can help pay off his debts. Please."

He breathes in sharply, his arms folding. "And what is it that you can do for me, Brooke?"

"You know what I'm capable of. More than most people."

"I do," he says, "but that doesn't change the fact that Jordie lost a lot of money. I'm barely asking for half."

She feels a scraping in her chest. "I get that, but I don't want to lose him. Something must have happened."

"Yeah, your boyfriend is a fucking idiot."

Hard to disagree in the present conversation.

"What can I do to fix this?" she asks.

"You were capable of disposing of the one man you should have loved most, so how can I trust you?"

She bites her lip. The past was buried and dead. Jared, Jordie, and herself were the only three people on earth that knew the truth.

Now, with Jordie's life obviously hanging in the balance,

she's willing to do anything to protect him.

"I never got to properly thank you for that," she says.

"No, you didn't," he says. "I don't know how Jordie got away and managed to dump the car, but he should have kept driving."

"Was the car damaged?"

"I don't know," he says and exhales sharply. "They aren't exactly calling me to let me know its condition, and Jordie hasn't said much either."

"I can't believe he didn't tell me," she says. "Seriously. What the fuck."

"If he were anybody else, this would already be over," Jared says matter-of-factly.

"I'll do anything to stop that from happening," she says. "Anything."

His tongue shows on the back of his teeth as he thinks. "Really, anything?" He walks toward her, placing his hands on her shoulders. "That's the girl I remember. That's the girl I'd consider making a deal with."

She tenses as he touches her, the next breath she draws shallow.

When Brooke was eighteen, before she had Jordie, when all she had was a deadbeat father and small prospects, Jared had managed to help her feel safe, or at least, less unsafe.

"What are you doing?" she asks as his hand moves from her shoulder to trail down her tank top, his index finger trailing the outline of her breasts.

"Seeing if you remember the girl that I protected five years ago," he says, taking her hand and placing it on his waist. "Do you?"

"And what about Jordie?" she asks.

"You still need to figure out a way to pay off his debts—I'm still pissed off," he says. "But I'll consider an extension as an act of good faith."

"So, you'll let me work for you?" she asks.

Jared shakes his head for a moment, his own hand cupping hers. "Yeah, I'll find something for you to do."

Jordie'll have to forgive her. If he can't, then at least he'll be alive to hate her.

"It seems like I'm always the one you come to when things are a mess," he says.

True. Why, she's not so sure.

"So, why do you help me?"

He laughs, then leans in to whisper in her ear, "I'm a sucker for a lost cause."

Jared, a man who takes everything he wants without hesitation, grabs her with both of his strong hands and pulls her to him, his eyes watching her.

He presses his lips against hers. She should feel guiltier as she kisses back, but Jordie is everything to her, and she's going to get him out of this mess.

Yet there's also a part of her that missed the fervour that overcomes her when Jared is involved.

She kisses him back, using her hands to unbutton his jeans. His hands move down her back and pull off her small tank top.

For a moment she's 18 again, and Jared is the older badass. The dangerous man who could give her the world, and maybe he'd have offered if she had given him a chance.

He turns her around, pushing her against his office wall and kissing the nape of her neck. It's hard to think any further.

For a selfless act of heroism, she sure is enjoying this.

Maybe she's a little angry that Jordie didn't tell her about their financial problems. And that he's a total idiot and made her have to come back to Jared in the first place. Maybe she's a little angry that Amanda's back in town too.

His hands ball up her hair as she turns to kiss his lips.

Maybe she just wants to do this.

Chapter 25: Amanda

Amanda spent most of the morning with Ryder. He was showing her various maneuvers for street racing, and he's explained to her the importance of shifting. It's nothing like the track her father let her drive as a teenager

Now, late-afternoon, she's finally behind the wheel. They've driven two hours away from the city, to an area with less traffic to bother them.

"You're not so bad," he says to her from the passenger seat, chomping on a burger from a fast food joint he'd insisted they drive through.

"Thanks," she says as they make a turn onto another back street. The weight of her wrist after driving all day causes her to wince. Her grip on the steering wheel with her right hand loosens, fingers numb and tingling.

Ryder watches her, eyes narrowed. "Are you okay?" he asks.

Amanda nods, "Yeah, I just need a break," she says as she pulls off into the parking lot of a community center.

"Why are you wincing?" he asks.

"It's just my wrist," she says. "Sometimes this happens."

She turns off the engine and leans back, resting her head on the seat. Most days she can forget there's a problem. Everything is normal. On other days, she can hardly lift a pen, or she'll drop something without even realizing that her grip had been lost.

"What happened to your wrist?"

"A year and a half ago, I injured it on a lift," she says. "It's mostly functional, but there's nerve damage."

"Natalie mentioned that you quit cheerleading and then college," he says facing her, face more solemn than she's used to. "Is this why?"

She nods her head once and affirms, "Yeah."

"You couldn't cheerlead anymore?" he asks.

"Maybe I could have," she says. "I probably could have figured something out if I did physio hard enough or if I really worked for it."

"But?" he asks.

"When I was injured, instead of feeling fear for my career or for the sport," she pauses for a moment to yawn, still exhausted from being up early, then says, "I just felt relief."

Cheerleading was her mother's idea. She liked it well enough, but it was never a plan for the future.

"But what about school?" he asks.

"I don't know. I just… didn't really see any of it as important," she says. "Did you go to school?"

"I did," he says, arm across the open window.

It hadn't occurred to her to ask Natalie what Ryder had been doing since she last saw him. To be honest, she'd kind of just thought he played around in his garage all day, slaving over his car and spending all of his free time racing.

It's not like they'd used to talk about the future.

"Well, for what?" she asks, adjusting her seat to reclining.

"Business management," he says, wiping his other hand on his jeans and continues, "with a double major in math."

She turns her head to stare at him, eyes wide. Face scrunched. She can't help it. "Are you kidding?" she asks.

He shrugs. "No, I'm not kidding."

"I didn't expect..."

"What?" he says, letting out a quick laugh, then asks, "That I'm smart?"

"I didn't say that," she says.

It's not really a surprise that Ryder's smart; it's more a surprise that he's even bothering with street racing.

"So, why are you still here?" she asks. "Shouldn't you be working on Wall Street or something?"

He shakes his head. "Can't stand suits."

"Then what do you do?" she asks.

"Right now, I'm running my dad's business," he says. "After he died, there was really nobody to run it, and it had a steady income."

"I'm sorry about your father," she says.

"Thanks," he says, but his face isn't a good indicator of his emotions.

"Did your dad race?"

He laughs. "Not a chance. He was way too controlled for that. But he did have good taste. He told me I could have the Supra if I worked with him as a teenager."

"So, he didn't pay you?"

"The Supra was payment enough," he says.

"How do you still have time for racing?" she asks. "Aren't you pretty busy?"

"No social life," he says. "Plus, somebody has to beat Jordie."

She laughs, watching his face. Taking note of the way he smiles with the corner of his mouth. How he's always freshly shaven.

She's surprised how much she likes spending time with Ryder.

Chapter 26: Natalie

"I'll make you a bet," Ben says.

The summer heat slaps against her skin, and she adjusts her bra straps as he talks.

"I didn't bring that much cash," she says. "Trying to cut back."

Ben shakes his head. "I don't want cash."

"What do you want?" she asks, her eyes wandering the crowd to see who has shown up for the competition. The cash part was mostly a lie; she had brought some of her savings just in case a race she couldn't refuse turned up. Particularly, a race that she knew she could win. Easy money for bills, especially the student debt that pretty much screams at her whenever she looks at her bank account.

"If I win, we spend the night together."

"Are you kidding me?" she asks, playing off like she's

insulted, but part of her is intrigued.

Street racing may have been about the cars at first, but as time has passed, the racing itself became more enjoyable. Particularly racing Ben. When they were together, they hadn't made a show of it or ever really shown interest in front of others, but they had raced. Racing Ben, especially the tug and pull of who might win, had become the best aphrodisiac she had yet to find.

"And what do I get if I win?" she asks.

"Whatever you want," Ben says. "You could have me."

She pretends to gag, but Ben leans in and says, "Come on, there's a good chance you'll win."

"Okay, fine, but if I win, I want you to stop calling me—I want nothing."

His face sinks, obviously regretting the playful challenge. "Really?" he asks.

"Yep," she says. "Besides, I'm not a commodity."

"No," he says. "But you still have feelings for me. Last week—"

"Was a mistake," she says. "But I'll take your bet."

If she wins, she finally gets peace of mind and gets to push Ben away from her for a while. She knows he'd crack and break the truce eventually, but his pride would at least give her a couple of weeks of silence. And if she loses? Well, she can think of worse things than the best sex of her life.

"Are you sure?" he asks as though he's reconsidered. "I don't want to pressure you."

"I'm sure," she says, and really, she is.

***

Behind the wheel of the Chevelle, she holds her breath. Ben's probably a jerk for suggesting the bet, but after her lapse in judgement last week, she's been thinking about him more a little too often. Like his lips on her thigh. And her breasts.

Ben's Charger rumbles, and the Chevelle follows suit. She turns her head to look at Ben, and he's looking at her too, eyes hungry.

She smirks at him, tightens her grip on the wheel, and presses her foot just above the gas.

The race starts, and their cars push forward, the weight shoving her head against the seat. The Charger is strong, and she lets Ben lead for a few seconds before she even bothers to pass him, but he moves quickly on the corner and pushes her to the inner corner, coming out of it and blazing a half of a second ahead. It doesn't take her too long to push the Chevelle next to him. She can't look into the next car; if she does, she'll lose focus on the race. But it's hard not to think of her bet, the stakes.

She catches a glimpse of him in the other car, biting his lip, strong hands gripping the wheel.

The adrenaline is intoxicating. They keep racing, sheets of metal and speed between them, but this is the closest she's felt to anybody in weeks.

It doesn't take long before they're back at the start-finish line, having spent most of the race flipping who's in the lead. With less than two seconds left in the race, she knows she's ready to win his silence. Except seeing him there, in the car, makes their history fade away. And just like that, he's the boy that kissed her in the library again, looking devilishly handsome, leaning in and whispering into her ear, always staring back at her like she's the only person in the world. Even if she doesn't want him back, it can't hurt to spend just another night with him.

She eases her foot off the gas just enough that Ben passes her with only a few inches until she reaches the line too.

Chapter 27: Axel

Lurking at street races watching Jordie and his friends is about as entertaining as hanging out at a high school dance. It's not like he even has friends around to blow off steam. So, he's sitting in his motel room trying to brainstorm ways to leave the country.

And thinking about leads.

Mostly the first one because this job teeters between life-endangering and being as dull as worn-down sandpaper.

When his handler asks to meet, they discuss the same loop of information. Barely anything new. Jared and Edge aren't moving much. From what he can tell, there has yet to be any visible fallout from the car bust. Silence is the worst-case scenario.

That means nothing has been planned yet.

At least if there had been action, he could plan, prepare,

find a way forward. He's poking around and waiting at the corner, just waiting to see if he'll be the cat or the mouse.

He's had too much time to think about his life. About every choice that's gotten him here. His family's money wasn't enough for him. He needed to do something for himself. He was the noble type, taking on causes—a crusader.

Now what is he? Trapped in some dive motel, waiting for the mafia to catch a glimpse of his face and I.D. him as a man to dispose of.

He thinks of his brother, Liam; gambling addict turned business mogul. Even the failure of his family had turned it all around and got his shit together. Hell, his divorced sister with two kids, Lorrie, even seems happy. Then again, she might just be happy that she's finally rid of Jamie and the rest of the Connors.

He's not necessarily depressed, he just figured that this job would mean something. Anything more than the shitshow it had turned into lately. All the more reason to finally catch a break. He could just arrest Jordie and take him in. He's wanted for drug trafficking, and he could permanently stop him from being a smug brat.

That's not going to fix his problem, though. Sure, Jordie is an arrogant, street-racing, drug-running, idiot, but he's reasonably sure that he's not that high up and that these runs aren't that frequent.

Far as he can tell, most of Jordie's activities involve racing and being gambled with. Not a huge catch. And if he's not talking now, he can't imagine locking him up is going to change much. Drug running doesn't seem to be his main gig, but nonetheless, he did end up in the Mercedes.

So far, his only leverage seems to be the girlfriend, Brooke.

He had pieced together her story from the little evidence he had gathered. Asked some questions and found more questions.

Neighbours from her childhood home confirmed that the last time they saw either Brooke or her father, Aaron, a fight incurred. Loud screaming, shattering glass, and then one loud popping sound.

The neighbour remembered being concerned because he thought Brooke, the teenager, might have been hurt. But, when he saw two men, one Aaron's age and the other young, maybe her boyfriend, he thought he had heard something else—maybe a car backfiring.

Except it was odd because they were loading luggage into a car. Maybe Brooke was moving out.

Then Aaron never came back either.

So, he had chalked it up to them moving away; people do that, and it wasn't a particularly safe neighbourhood. He explained to Axel that he was used to neighbours coming and going.

And maybe Aaron moving out would have been plausible except nobody had heard from him at his construction job either; though they'd mentioned he had shown up drunk a few times and was on his last leg. The foreman remembered him and said he'd assumed Aaron had just kept drinking and decided not to bother coming back.

He assumed if he kept digging, it would continue going in the same direction. Aaron was gone, Brooke was still here. He was starting to build a picture, and he was going to look for more info, but really, Jordie revealed more than any sleuthing could have.

He was stirred up when Axel mentioned Brooke's father, and even more so, he knew something. Axel was reasonably sure he'd found the young man that was outside of the house the night Aaron was last seen.

Chapter 28: Brooke

4 Years Ago

They say girls are doomed to be their mothers. She is doomed to be her father. At least, she's doomed to be like her father in some ways.

Always tripping over what the right or wrong answer is and finding herself in some moral grey area. Doomed to repeat mistakes and fall back into the trap of survival.

She's just doing what she needs to do.

Going forward the only way she knows how.

Not all of her decisions are good ones. But that's the curse.

We are who raised us.

Even if we're actively trying not to be.

Her father stands before her, holding a beer bottle, cursing. He's been in a bad mood all day.

At 18, it's time for her to leave home.

It's time to walk away from his miserable self and finally start living.

Ever since he'd moved home, her childhood friend, Jordie, has been encouraging her to walk away. To run from this mess and finally move on.

Her father is a washed-up alcoholic and has been ever since her mom left Brooke with him.

Jesus, Aaron, could you be more cliché?

Both of her parents are selfish.

So, maybe she is like her mother a bit because she's packed her bags, and they're by the door. She's not going to take another minute of his shit. Aaron can do his own laundry, cook his own food, and drink himself to death in the decrepit 2 room shack that somebody had the sense of humor to call a house.

"Where do you fucking think you're going?" he asks, stumbling as he moves forward. "I'm hungry. Make my dinner."

Jordie texts her, and she checks her phone in between the grumbling. *Still want me to come?* he asks.

Jordie is coming to pick her up. He has a cousin who'll let her stay a few nights. Get on her feet. Figure out a place that she can stay from there.

Yes, she replies quickly, her eyes darting from the phone to her father. *Come get me.*

She pockets her phone.

Aaron's eyes are dark, his white shirt stained with pasta sauce from the dinner she made him the night before.

Bottles line the coffee table, the counter, and the kitchen

table.

Some would say he'd been on a bender. In reality, he's merely on his regular Friday which has melted over to Wednesday.

Her breathing is shallow, but she steadies herself. "I'm leaving. Make your own dinner."

"You ungrateful bitch," he says, still stumbling, shaking the beer bottle in his trembling hand. "What, you're going to go like your whore mother did?"

She bites her lip, mentally begging Jordie to drive as fast as he can. The last thing she needs is another bruise.

"I'm 18, it's time for me to move out."

"Who will take care of me?" he asks. "I took care of you when she left—you owe me."

Yeah, fuck your mental gymnastics, Aaron.

"I am your daughter, that's the job," she says, readying herself to grab her bags and wait outside. "And you did a shit job of it, by the way."

"What did you say to me?" he asks, flinging the bottle from his hand and lurching toward her.

His aim is slightly off; the bottle makes an impact on the cinderblock wall behind her head, exploding into hundreds of tiny pieces and blowing glass across the tiny, grungy room.

She can't take any more of this. She reaches into her purse and fumbles for the slim metal object that Jared had given her for protection. For the next time that Aaron threatened her.

She removes the safety like he had shown her, and Aaron

laughs at her.

He taunts her, "What are you going to do with that?" he asks, and he takes a step toward her.

She doesn't respond with words. Instead, she presses her finger on the trigger. The shot is so loud, so disorienting, that she's not sure what happens next. Not clearly.

Aaron falls to the floor, and pools of red beginning to seep through his shirt.

Chapter 29: Natalie

The morning light floods in through the window, the curtains left open from the night before. She rolls over, slightly disoriented, before she realizes that she's in Ben's bed. He's lying next to her, still asleep, pretty much smiling. There's a taste in her mouth like acid. She had never meant to stay; she must have fallen asleep pretty quickly after because she doesn't remember much. Except his tongue in her mouth, the way her legs felt wrapped around him, and the deep sighs that lasted for much longer than she had expected.

She feels almost hungover as she rolls out of the bed. Ben groans and reaches out in his sleep—reaching for her.

She stands quickly and looks back at him in the bed. He looks so sweet and innocent, only half-covered by the grey duvet. Asleep, he looks like the boy she had met. The boy who was full of promise, ready to take on the world and conquer it with the law degree he hoped to obtain. The boy who loved politics and even seemed to think that the world could be a better place. His apartment has some holdouts from that time. His large bookshelf still houses Plato's *Republic* and numerous academic works. Some are leather-bound, and they're mostly in pristine condition. Thinking of the drug dealer and mob lackey he's become is too much contrast with the boy that has these books.

She takes one into her hands, not sure why, but she wants to touch the Ben that existed three years ago. She leafs through the pages and sees his notes; small, perfect printing in the margins. One might think that they were typed additions to the book; they're so concise and well-placed.

Ben stirs, so she quickly closes the book and puts it back carefully, sure that it's in the exact position it was before she touched it.

"Good morning," Ben says, pulling the remainder of the covers off of him, revealing that he's still undressed.

"Morning," she says softly in return, still not sure why she hasn't left.

"Come back to bed," he says, almost begging.

She shakes her head. "I've got work."

His face turns to disappointment, but he shakes it off and stretches. "Come on, one more hour," he says, trying his best to sound enticing.

She wants to. She'd like to curl back up in that bed forever with him, in a time and place where everything else melts away. Unfortunately, that's not how the world works.

They can never get back what they once were, even if brief lapses of judgement threaten to peel away at the barrier she's been building.

"I'm sorry," she says, "but I really do need to go."

She grabs her shorts and her black tank top and puts them on hastily. Not even trying to fiddle with the bra, she throws it in her purse. They had driven there separately, so her car is waiting for her downstairs. The last thing she needed was an excuse to spend more time with Ben, so she's glad he's not driving her home.

Ben gets out of bed and puts on boxer shorts. "At least let me hug you goodbye," he says.

He walks the short distance across the room and wraps his arms around her. She tries to resist, but his soft scent is hard to ignore. She lets him hug her and even accepts the small kiss he places on her lips.

"This was the last time," she says.

He nods and doesn't say what they're both thinking. *You say every time is the last time.* The unspoken words hang over them, but she's convinced she's going to try and make this the final last time. For real.

Chapter 30: Amanda

She has run out of excuses for her driving anxiety. If she's going to street race, it's time to actually try. She inhales. For her first race, she'd like the competition to be friendly. Getting her ass kicked is going to feel less pathetic when it's by a friend.

"Ryder, you got yourself another groupie?" a short guy with no hair asks with a strong Spanish accent.

He isn't ugly or menacing looking, but his face is round and looks sort of like Pitbull. He stands next to a friend who's nearly as white as snow with the blonde hair to match. They look a bit like sidekicks to some movie villain.

The blonde laughs.

Ryder looks like he's about to answer, but Amanda shakes her head at him and faces the guy who's been kind enough to judge her.

"Excuse me," she smiles sweetly, "is there a problem?"

The guy laughs in her face and says something in Spanish. The only word she can make out is *chiquita.* The other guy responds in a broken accent, and they chuckle.

"I'm just a guy who likes pretty things; cars, women, blondes," he emphasizes the words with his voice as though his accent could cover his misogyny.

Ryder, not laughing, has his arms crossed. He looks ready to speak, but Natalie approaches, pretty much drifting into the conversation from God knows where.

"Eric," she says, "give her a break," then says something in Spanish that must be an insult because Eric tenses and nods.

The name Eric is familiar; Natalie had mentioned him owning a garage, supplying parts, and being the reason that Ryder and Natalie got involved in the first place. He looks to be mid-forties. It's kind of pathetic that this is his entire life, but she doesn't say that.

Ryder is laughing.

She's not sure if she should laugh, thank Natalie, or run off like a scared animal.

She hopes the comment was a dig at his brown corduroy shorts with a lime green polo shirt. He looks like he belongs in a geriatric ward.

"I'm not here to chase racers around like a lost puppy dog," she raises her car keys, shakes them, and points to the Subaru.

The two guys laugh, but the friend doesn't say very much. He's probably a complete moron.

"You're going to race that little, dinky toy?"

She's fine with him insulting her whether that be her clothes or her hair, but her WRX is beautiful.

"Hey, I put a lot of work into that car," Natalie folds her arms. "Watch yourself."

"Eric, get lost," Ryder says with exasperation.

"I just want to race like everybody else," Amanda says.

"Sure, why not. It might be fun to watch you get your ass kicked," Eric chuckles and then bobs his ugly head. "Free entertainment."

"Whatever," she says.

Natalie decides now is the best time to laugh, then says something to him in Spanish.

Eric grumbles back, still speaking Spanish, then walks away. His blonde friend complies and follows him.

"What did you say?" she asks Natalie who is smirking in Eric's absence.

Ryder shakes his head. "She reminded him that the last race he won was in 2002."

"They don't respect me, and they never will," Amanda says as she sighs. The same reason she could never be a professional driver. Nobody is going to believe that the ex-cheerleader is worthy of, or even able to, drive.

"Why do you need their respect?" Ryder asks, shrugging.

As though respect doesn't matter. She almost huffs. "I don't know. Why don't you want to lose to Jordie? Self-respect."

"I guess so, but I still don't see why you'd waste your time thinking about what those idiots think," he says as he walks to the Supra a few paces away, then reaches into the car to grab something.

"He's right, you know," Natalie says, hovering over Ryder and the Supra. "They'll know you're a good driver when you prove it. Everything else is just *pretense.*"

Ryder stands and hands her a small coin. It's not an American coin—Mexican maybe.

"What's this for?"

"Good luck," Natalie says. "I gave this to Ryder the first time he raced. He thought it was the stupidest idea ever."

Amanda presses her index finger on the coin in her palm. "So, why give it to me?" she asks.

"Because I won," he says.

She reaches into her jean pocket and drops the coin, releasing her hand. "Thank you."

Natalie stares Amanda in the face with a deadpan expression and says, "I hope you lose because I plan on winning."

Without saying another word, she walks off to the Chevelle.

"Good luck," Ryder says, leaning in to whisper near her ear. "Even though you're the competition."

"Thanks," is all she manages to get out before the man she'd seen at the last race shouts that it's time to get into their cars. She shivers with anticipation. This is the moment that she's been waiting for since she gave up everything.

Slower than usual, she gets into the car and adjusts herself behind the wheel. She feels the steering wheel beneath her fingers.

She allows herself twenty seconds to freak out. Within those seconds, she breathes heavily, shakes her head, and contemplates crying. As soon as they're up, she takes a deep breath and puts her car into gear, moving to the start-finish line.

Ten seconds and ten years feel like they pass all at once as she waits for the race to start. Then, the cars lurch forward. Tires squeal as they go from static to jolting forward, accelerating to speeds well past the posted speed limit.

All of her attention is on her car. The weight. The speed. The tumultuousness that accompanies that speed.

As long as she doesn't hit anything or take the turns too sharp, she should be fine.

The speed remains constant as they smoothly sprint down the blacktop. Her heart is pounding faster than it should.

It's liberating to push the car to the fastest speed possible. No need to control the speedometer—only force the car past its own limitations, past the limitations of the law.

Besides herself, Natalie, Ryder, Ben, and an unidentified Civic are in the race.

Ben pushes beside her, passing the WRX as though she were driving the speed limit. She's not surprised, but she's still frustrated.

Her only concern is her hands on the steering wheel and keeping her car straight. The last thing she wants to do is get distracted. All the practice in the world isn't enough to prepare you for hurling metal death machines speeding side by side, all after the same goal.

She presses her gas pedal harder. If she holds her foot down anymore, it might snap off at the ankle, but she doesn't let up.

Turning her attention back to the cars ahead of her, she can see Ryder and Ben fighting for the leading position. Ben's trying to push Ryder out of the way, but Ryder doesn't budge. There's something about the way he drives that's both calm and fearless—certainly different than the reckless nature of Ben who nearly spins himself out.

She begs the Subaru to go faster but meets her limit and eases off the gas a little bit. The Civic is a few feet behind her, but he's not tailgating. They come up on a turn, and Amanda keeps the WRX steady as she takes it on the inside. It's stressful trying to keep her mind at ease as she watches the wall of a building that she could easily scrape into draw nearer. Her breath is heavy.

Perhaps the oddity is that she's more concerned about the driver behind her than she is the buildings.

The Civic makes the turn a little wide and almost passes her, but she speeds up enough that he can't quite make it. Sweat is building on her forehead.

Coming out of the turn, she can assess the race.

Ryder has managed to pass Ben even if only by a few seconds.

Natalie, who for some reason was near last most of the race, has come from behind the Civic and is now side-by-side with Amanda.

Amanda breathes in, shifts the car, and presses the gas down, getting just enough of a boost that she manages to cross the finish line in third after Ryder and Ben.

She thinks of the coin in her pocket. She may not have

won, but third is better than fifth, so she'll take it.

***

"Good race, Amanda," Ryder says, and he actually seems impressed by her. She smiles happily.

"You're the one who had the good race. Nice job beating Ben," she says.

"Fuck off, bitch," Ben interjects as he walks past them. "I'm just surprised you know how to use a clutch."

Natalie, emerging from her car a little later than the others, looks frustrated as she approaches Ben.

"Leave her alone," she says, sitting on Ryder's car.

Ryder doesn't say much; just watches them all, glaring, like he's adrenaline high from his win.

Ben shrugs and looks at them nonchalantly. "I was just paying the bottle-head blonde a compliment. Not often I see a girl who knows how to drive a car."

Natalie scoffs. "Yeah, I get it, you're mad at me."

He shakes his head at her. "I'm not mad at you. You made your position *pretty fucking clear.*"

"What position?" Amanda asks.

Natalie shakes her head. "It doesn't matter," she says.

Ryder seems uninterested in their drama and turns to talk to some of the other drivers, discussing the current build of the Supra.

Ben and Natalie share a look. Amanda can't discern what the look is or what it means, so she turns her head, trying to give them some space.

After a few moments, she hears Natalie say, "Bye," and then whisper something under her breath in Spanish.

When she turns back to look, Ben is walking away.

"What was that about?" Amanda asks.

Natalie shakes her head. "Same old drama, different day," she sighs. "Good job, by the way."

Amanda smiles, still proud of her first attempt. "Thanks."

Ryder, turning his attention from the other drivers, looks to Natalie. "What was that? I've never seen you drive that bad."

Natalie folds her arms. "Can't win them all, right?"

He nods. "That's true, but I can."

Amanda has to laugh, but to be fair, Ryder had just won. "I think your good luck charm helped me," she says, reaching into her pocket to retrieve it and give it back.

He shakes his head. "Nah, keep it."

"Are you sure?" she asks.

He smirks, then says, "I clearly didn't need it."

Natalie looks at them both, then moves her eyes through the crowd. "I'm going to go," she says, then turns to Ryder, "I'll see you at home."

"Okay," he says.

Amanda nods, saying, "See you later."

Natalie leaves quickly. Amanda's too buzzed from the race to think about why or to question further.

"How do you feel?" Ryder asks.

"Honestly?" she says, "High."

He laughs and nods. "Same."

She can hear music playing from a few of the cars and feels the last bits of anxiety flow away. Whatever reasons she has to race, they've floated away too, replaced by the endorphin rush.

"I don't want to go home yet," she says. "Can we race again?"

"You could, but I don't know if you want to push your beginner's luck that hard," he says.

Chapter 31: Axel

Hat down over his head, Axel is sitting across from Jonny in the back booth of an Irish pub. He would have preferred this meeting to be more private, but Jonny was worried that meeting in the motel would have linked them together. He'd had to drive for three hours just to meet him.

He's exhausted, but the pub has just enough humming noise that nobody will overhear them.

Jonny, his long-term partner and friend, had somehow managed to be his handler on this case. The heads probably thought Jonny was the only one that could keep him in check. They have a history, and maybe that history would be enough to pry the truth out of him.

So, like a traitor, Jonny sits across from him nursing his scotch, sipping like it's his only job in the world.

"I don't have anything yet," he says to Jonny.

His own drink is untouched.

"I figured," Jonny says and nods, the slightest remnants of a southern accent in his voice. "But they're restless. You have to figure something out."

Two men pass them by, and Jonny makes a remark about the basketball on the widescreen television. For some reason, he thinks about laughing at the thought of the dusty-haired southern boy drinking Scotch whisky in an Irish pub.

The men leave, and Axel grasps his whiskey and brings it to his lips, taking a gulp. He holds the glass in hand as he talks in a low voice, "I know."

Jonny has a file folder in front of him that he pushes toward Axel. "I looked into that girl you told me about," he says, placing his now empty glass on the table.

"And?" Axel asks.

"You said her father went missing when she was 18," Jonny says, flipping through the file to bring out a photograph. "We didn't have anything on her, but Aaron is another story."

"As far as I can tell, Aaron was nothing more than an alcoholic and a flake; I'm sure he has some priors," Axel says, stopping to finish his drink before he continues. "Petty thievery? Hit and run?"

Jonny shakes his head, handing him some photos from the folder. In the dim light of the pub, it takes him a few seconds to focus, squinting at first. Crime scene photos of two men dead in pools of their own blood, gunshot wounds to their heads.

"You think this was Aaron?" he asks.

Jonny shakes his head. "I know it was. There was a DNA match, but they never found Aaron."

"Is that all?"

"No, he was also friends with Jared's father, Lorenzo, back when he was in power," Jonny says. "It looks like the mob runs in Brooke's blood."

Axel holds the photo still, analysing the scene. "Yeah, and so does murder."

Chapter 32: Natalie

She dances feverishly, swaying her body to the beat of one of the few Latin-styled clubs in the city.

Her skin is hot and sweaty as she moves to the beat of the Spanish beat mixed with urban lyrics. Her heart pumps, and she sways. The man on her arm, she's never met before, but he's wearing golden chains proudly—Puerto Rican maybe.

It doesn't matter.

The summer heat flashes through the club, bodies grinding together as the music drums louder.

Flashing lights and a psychedelic intoxication that keeps her moving along to the music—one song through the next, the beats fading into one another.

Her hips flow side to side as his hands rest on her back.

She feels breathless, still moving to the beat.

Anything to keep her body moving.

Ever since she can remember, she can't handle standing still. She feels smothered when she has to stay in one position too long—with one person. One heart.

She was never meant to belong to somebody.

She tried to warn Ben that, but he couldn't be convinced. He thought he would be the gringo to tame her exotic heart, bring her back to his family and turn her into some 50s housewife.

If Ben knew anything about her, he'd have realized from day one that she wasn't going to be the wife of a laywer—go to PTA meetings and raise his insufferable bratty children. The kind of kids that think they never have to work or grind, that are too good for Chilaquiles.

Fucking kids that hang out with their white-washed, brainwashed, perfect amigos and smugly curse at their friends thinking they're all tough and shit because their daddy is a big-shot abogado.

Now he's tied to the mafia, and he's still trying to get with her. Infuriating, she thinks.

She keeps dancing, feeling the music as it moves through her. White boys don't dance the same. They clutch their shoulders together, and they cuck their bodies, or they go too far and they turn it into some kind of grinding session.

No, real dancing—that takes finesse.

The Latin boy is dipping her, pulling her with him, keeping her balanced as they turn the music into their own symphony.

If she didn't have family here, Ryder, her mother, she'd consider taking off. Maybe going to México and getting lost in some forgotten village by the sea. Why come back? she thinks. What is there here for her? It's not even political or religious. She just feels suffocated in the Chicago breezes.

Trapped in the confines.

Slowed down by the drudges of this modern life. She could leave. Fly through towns one by one, never settling down. Never really touching the ground.

All she really desires is to keep moving. Her Chevelle, just like her, is built to move. There's no stopping, no thinking about the next move, only the road.

Chapter 33: Ryder

"Where did you get these tickets from?" he says, trying to make small talk, but he wants to know. Tickets like these are at least $100 a piece, and the pit passes are even more.

"My dad always has some of them set aside in case I want them," Amanda says, and he shrugs like this isn't a big deal. Of course it wouldn't be a big deal to a girl who was raised in a house that has more square feet than the entire block he grew up on. He tries not to be bitter. It's not Amanda's fault her parents are rich.

"That's cool," he says. He doesn't want to insult her, so he keeps his comments to himself. It doesn't matter how they're going to the race; it only matters that they are. He needs to stop judging her for the high school version of herself. She's older now, and so is he.

"It is. He'll be there today."

Ryder's pulse quickens. He understands why Amanda is

dressed up, and he instantly feels like he's underdressed. Amanda should have added that her father was going to be there before she'd invited him on a daytrip. She probably held it back on purpose. He would have said no if he knew, and she probably foresaw his answer.

"Your father's going to be there?" He tries to mask the concern in his voice, but his eyes are having trouble. He keeps them focused on the road instead of looking over at Amanda. He doesn't know if he likes her, but now he has to meet her father. His grip tightens on the wheel, knuckles turning white.

"Yeah, don't worry about it. We'll only see him for a second, and then he has to work."

"Of course," he says. Big-business men wouldn't have time to stay for the entire race.

Amanda sits up straight and yawns. She looks over at him. "Can we stop at a fast food restaurant? I'm hungry."

"You want fast food?"

"Yeah, so?"

"I didn't take you for the type that eats junk," he finds it amusing that Amanda wants fast food; her image says all organic.

"Everybody eats this stuff sometimes, besides, I'm hungry."

He obliges. He's hungry too. Amanda orders an extra greasy, extra cheesy breakfast sandwich with a soda to drink. Even if it's grotesquely unhealthy to drink soda for breakfast, he gets one too. Sugar and caffeine might help ease the tension he's feeling.

He watches in amusement as Amanda licks the cheese off her lips. Every time he sees her, she manages to go against his expectation.

Once they arrive, Ryder paces his breathing and keeps his expression blank. Amanda looks vibrant as they walk around the grounds of the track. There are souvenir stands placed everywhere, and he considers getting a hat or something to bring home with him. He isn't the nostalgic type, but he hopes he'll remember this day for a while. He decides against the memento. It's too ridiculous and silly.

When Amanda goes toward the drivers' section, Ryder is uneasy. He loves racing, but it's weird seeing these drivers. It's also frustrating to be around a bunch of people who do it professionally. He assumes they think of street racers as total idiots, but he doesn't care. Racing is just as much his life as it is to any of these big shots—if not more. He's dedicated years of his time and effort to his car and had no team to perfect it. All of his triumphs are his own. He doesn't have millions of dollars in sponsorship.

Amanda braces herself for the reaction as she shows her badges to the security people who are running the backstage portion of the events. Hopefully her father will have enough time to see her and say hello. She knows he's busy, and she doesn't want to bother him, but she needs to see him. He needs to know that she took the time to go there. It's the first step in mending the fence she'd built by taking off. She needs her father more than anything.

The backstage has camera crews and interviewers setting up for the race. Some of the drivers are already doing pre-show reports. Amanda hasn't felt this at home in a long time—except behind the wheel of her car. As a child, she wandered around in places just like this, aimlessly, until her mother finally managed to wrangle her and drag her to meet strangers. Back then, she wore her hair in ribbons and pigtails.

She looks over at Ryder who is staring at the track in the distance. She wishes she could tell exactly what he's thinking, unless it was negative, then she'd rather not know. She wants to remember this day as a good one. A really good day.

She spots the driver for number 4, and her expression and mood warm instantly. It's been far too long since she's seen him in his race uniform and too long since she'd seen him at all. Amanda forgets that Ryder has no idea who her father is and walks up behind the racer and gives him a huge hug. He turns in confusion at first but smiles down at his daughter and hugs her back.

"Hey, sweetheart," he brings forward his arms to wrap Amanda in a larger hug and isn't bothered by the people watching them. Anybody who knows him knows he has children.

"Hey, Dad."

When Amanda glances at Ryder, she can't tell his emotions from his face. He should take up gambling. His poker face is perfect.

***

Ryder watches Amanda and her father interact. At first, he assumed she was just some crazy fan girl when she'd attacked the racer in front of them. He was worried they'd be kicked out by security.

Finding out he was her father confused him at first, but it put the missing pieces into place. He knew Amanda must have had more experience behind the wheel other than regular driving. She isn't a perfect street racer, but her style is a little too refined for a rebellious rich girl. It also explains why the father she talked about had spent so much time at a racetrack, but instead of being a stuffy executive, he's a driver. Ryder has to admit, he's a little impressed, but he doesn't show it. Racer aside, he's still meeting Amanda's father, and it's awkward. They aren't even dating, and they aren't even really friends.

Amanda turns his way and points to him. He doesn't know what's in store for him or if he should say something. "Dad, this is my friend Ryder. I thought I'd take him to the track."

Amanda's father—who she's yet to name, but he recognizes from TV appearances— extends his hand to Ryder, and he shakes it. Kevin Carson has been racing for as long as Ryder can remember, has won various championships, and continues to race in the sport. His interest in the legal racing world wasn't enough to let him now that Kevin also had a daughter, and a pretty one at that.

It dawns on him now that he's never even asked Amanda what her last name is. Even when he knew her as Jordie's girlfriend, he'd never taken the time to get to know even that much about her. Shit. She must think he's a jerk.

Ryder tries to muster a smile even though his mind is rushing forward at twenty miles per second. "It's nice to meet you," is all he can manage. He doesn't know what kind of guy her dad is. Is he strict? Or is he fun-loving? What do professional racers do in their free time? Galas? Or do they tinker with their cars?

Seeing Amanda next to her father, the professional stock car driver, paints an entirely different picture of her. She isn't just a girl that was raised around purses and shoes and yearned to rebel. She was raised around a track and watched the person she admired most win races and conquer the world behind an automobile. Becoming a street racer wasn't so much a lapse of judgement but more so a need to race too. He can imagine how hard it would have been for her to race legally. The media and the redneck morons that watch racing would have been all over her. Street racers are nothing compared to the scrutiny of the public eye. He thinks about Danica Patrick and the negative reflections she'd brought just for being a woman, and worse, pretty. He can imagine how a pretty little blonde would be treated.

Chapter 34: Natalie

"I had a shit day at work," Ben says, sipping rum out of a paper bag.

She reaches for the rum, taking it from him, and takes her own swig before handing it back.

"What happened?" she asks.

"Things are getting fucked with my boss," he says. "One cop pulls me over with a busted headlight, and Edge is accusing me of being a rat." He groans.

"So, Edge is acting like a lunatic? Isn't that kind of his thing?" she says, tapping her fingers on the rip of her black shorts.

"True," he says.

He places his hand on her thigh, and she considers moving it, but she doesn't. When he asked her to meet, she should have said no, but the part of her that can't shake him said yes, stupidly.

"You're hot," he says, eyes watching her like he wants to have sex with her on the park bench.

He probably would too—if she'd let him.

"I have to go," she says, watching him as he sips from the bottle.

"Where?" he asks.

"Somewhere with music," she says.

He nods and says, "Alright," then pauses before asking, "Do you want me to come?"

She shakes her head and says, "No."

He sighs, "But you'll still meet me next week, right?"

She wishes she could skip meeting him next week, but they both know that she'll be there, right on time, too.

"I'll be here," she says, watching him sip the rum on a park bench. She feels a bit sorry for him; he's always here, waiting, but all she can think of is leaving. Not just the bench, but the city.

Chapter 35: Brooke

When she thinks of her father—in the moments where the thought truly pangs at her heart, draws her breath from her chest, and sinks her to the kind of abyss that suffocates a person—it's never because of the bad moments.

She almost never thinks of the bitter ending or the bruises. Her mother leaving, the drinking. No, those moments are hidden in the back of her psyche, put away and almost never recovered.

The moments that suffocate her are always those that brought her joy. Memories that would be expressed with fondness in any other reality. Ice-cream as a child, outings, or family vacations in a simpler time. Hugs on good days. Warmth.

It is these good memories that remind her that the good always came with the bad, that there is no memory worth all the pain. Everything between them had been tarnished by the monstrosity that he had become—that he had made her become.

Whatever darkness that resides inside her was born from years of torment. It came to spite the good moments, lying in its wake, and eventually seeping through her veins until it poisoned all it touched.

Now, as she watches Jordie keep going through Jared's world, it's hard not to draw comparisons to her father. The night he came to get her, the night that they had become bonded through spilled blood—that of her father—was the night that she had passed on her burden and the darkness to him.

Perhaps she feels the pain so faintly because she knows somewhere inside that if she let it out, if she unleashed its grip, she may become lost inside herself, never to return. Jordie had always sheltered her from the brunt of the pain, and now with his life dangling before her eyes, she's not sure what help she can be.

She assumes there was a time when Aaron was more than a monster. When he was a man capable of love and compassion. The small collection of good memories that she hangs on to are devious reminders that every one of them—she, Jordie, Jared, Aaron—are all capable of making the decisions that eventually lead them to a spiralling doom.

Sitting alone at her kitchen table, Jordie gone off into the night to contend with Jared, or maybe his cop and his lies, she sloshes another shot of whiskey. Pours it back into her throat, lets it run all the way down without wincing. Tears welling in the sockets of her eyes, coming down her face.

A small moment of weakness within her tantalizing present. Even survivors sometimes feel the bitterness of the blades that once pierced their skin.

Besides, she's always been a little too solemn, broody, and capable of a depth of sadness. Jordie shields her from it as much as he can—stopped her from losing all of her senses the night she washed her father's blood from her hands. Wiping them clean over and over like the shadowy Lady Macbeth as she tried to reconcile what she had done. He had pulled her back, centered her in reality, and let her know that she had little other choice.

But she did have a choice.

We all have a choice.

The choice to take the hit, to stand firm as a moral statue. Or, even to tell the truth when the blow was settled. She could have told the cops. Risked whatever gavel a judge and jury would have her endure.

She made another choice.

And Jordie chose to help shelter her from that burden.

Now, she's sinking, and she's not sure if he'll be there as the wreckage capsizes.

Jordie may be stupid and irrational, but he'd done it all for her. And why? Under what universe is she anything worth sacrifice?

She worries, too, that she won't have the strength to save him because she's not sure she's going to be able to save herself.

Aaron may be dead and buried, but the cycle of tumultu-ousness and violence had not gone with him.

There was still Jared.

And her.

Jordie, in all his arrogance, may still be blind to the scope of the reality of their present, but she feels the same dis-cerning perception that led Bonnie Parker to write "The Trail's End".

Maybe Jordie isn't a cold-blooded killer, but she is. Just because she feels profound worry at the thought of Jordie being caught in a rabbit snare, that does not absolve her of guilt for removing Aaron from the earth.

To tell the truth, she doesn't feel guilt that he's dead.

She toasts the air before she slicks back another shot.

To Aaron, may you rot in hell.

Chapter 36: Amanda

She hadn't been home for longer than 40 minutes before Jordie's number popped across her screen, begging her to meet. Her better judgement tells her that she should ignore him. Jordie is a grown adult, perfectly capable of making his own decisions. Her better judgement was ignored, and now Jordie is sitting next to her on the front stoop of her building.

"What happened to you?" she asks Jordie.

He shakes his head like he doesn't know what she means. "I'm the same person I've always been."

Amanda has to look up at him to close the near foot of height he has on her. His hair is out of place, and his shirt is dirty. Jordie may have always been reckless, but he was never dishevelled.

"No, something is going on with you," she says, unwavering.

Jordie swallows and peers down at her, his eyes showing a little bit of the misery that he's obviously trying to poorly hide.

"I'm in trouble," he says.

Trouble. Jordie's always been a street racer since she's known him. Fast, wild, free. Roaming the streets without a cause.

"You're in trouble?" she asks, then tries to laugh to cut the tension before saying, "I thought you were *the* trouble."

"Both," he says, then closes his mouth and looks toward the sky.

She questions what could be so severe that he doesn't even want to look her in the eyes. What mistake could be bad enough that Jordie is finally showing shame? It's not like he ever apologized for the Brooke debacle.

"I really fucked up this time," he says.

She raises her eyebrows.

"Yeah, but you're not saying how you fucked up," she says and then sighs.

He raises his cuffed fist to his chin, pressing it there like he's in pain. He winces, and it starts to scare her.

Her Jordie, the boy she had fallen for, wasn't wavering. He was an arrogant son of a bitch and kind of an adrenaline junkie, but he wasn't afraid of anything. Actually, he made a point not to be.

"It can't be that bad if you're still here," she says.

He opens his mouth as though he's offended. The way people do when somebody doesn't understand the full scope of a disaster, like lamenting a storm for not being too bad because your house was fine but actually your neighbour's is totalled.

"That's the thing," Jordie says, finally looking her in the eyes, his hand moving from his chin. "I'm not sure how long I'll be here."

"Why?" she asks, her hand moving to push her hair from her face. Her weight shifts from one foot to another. "Are you going to run away?"

The thought of Jordie being gone is polarizing. Sure, she hates him for breaking her heart, but he's still the first person she ever loved, ever slept with, hell, the first person that made her feel anything other than a cut-out of a person.

"Run," he says, placing his hand on her arm, "or run out of time."

His hand on her arm sparks electricity. Even here, even now. After every ounce of pain that he's put her through. The match is still lit. Lighters don't care if they've burned down houses; they just burn when ignited.

"Are you going to tell me what you're talking about?" she asks, her voice a bit sharper.

She can't help it.

He's touching her, and it's shaking her to her core. She doesn't know if she should push him away or pull him in and comfort him.

Plus, he's kind of scaring her.

His head jerks to the side, bloodshot eyes with dilated pupils scanning the area.

Looking for somebody in particular. He's real nervous,

like the guys in movies she's seen—the ones that know they're being watched or a part of some big conspiracy. Or completely burnt out.

"Are you on drugs?" she blurts out.

"What?" he asks, drawing it out, voice a little louder than before, dropping his hand from her arm to his side. "Why do you think I'm on drugs?"

"I don't know," she says, thinking it over for a second. "I guess you're kind of acting like you're on drugs."

"I'm not on drugs," he says, voice flat, measured.

"Then why are you so paranoid?" she asks.

He groans, eyes now on her.

"You're not going to drop this, are you?" he asks.

She shakes her head. Nope. Not a chance. Even though it's not her mess to clean up. She checked out of that problem the day he took off. But that doesn't mean she doesn't care.

He opens the passenger door of the Judge, motioning with his left hand. "Get in, then."

"Where are we going?" she asks.

"I just want to drive. It helps me think," Jordie says.

To be honest, she's still not entirely sure he's not completely fucked up on Adderall or something fringe and random. Jordie strikes her as the type that's not going to do your normal street drugs. Nope, he's too cool for that. He's going to do something ironic or something he found in his mother's drug cabinet when he visited her for the weekend. Maybe Prozac. Whatever the upper-middle-class ladies who wear pearls and attend tennis matches are swallowing nowadays.

"I'm not even sure you're sober," she says, making a point to look inside the car to see if there are any pill bottles lying around. "Why would I get in the car with you?"

He groans at her, making a loud 'ugh' sound.

"Amanda, do you want to know what's going on or not?" he says, pushing the door so that it's fully open. "I'm completely sober, I promise."

She nods, "Yeah, okay."

She walks toward the Judge a little timidly. She did just accuse its driver of being completely burnt out even though he probably is. But she wants to know what's going on, so she gets in the car.

Jordie slams the door behind her, and she jolts up, disorientated for a moment before reaching for the seatbelt and clasping it closed, testing it and ensuring it's safe as Jordie walks around the car and gets in.

If he is high, she at least wants to make sure she's going to survive.

It's not like she's anti-drug; she's just anti-car-plus-drug. Anti-death too. Plus, Jordie's good at street racing and illegal driving. She wouldn't necessarily let him drive her hypothetical children to school.

So, it's probably good he left her before they ever had kids.

He starts the engine, and they take off a little too fast. She doesn't mind the speed. What she minds is that the car is super muggy and humid in the summer heat. She rolls down the window, noticing empty wrappers strewn across the back seat from the corner of her eye.

"Your car's a mess," she says.

"I've been in it a lot," he replies. His hands gripping the wheel for dear life. "I've been going for drives alone. Trying to think."

"Think about what?" she asks, her eyes now on the road, watching the world float by them as they speed past commercial lots.

It's hard not to feel sixteen again.

Same car.

Same boy.

Different story.

"That guy you saw me talking to at the race," he says, making a turn toward an area she's not familiar with. "He's a cop."

She holds her hands together, squeezing them as she processes. "So, what? You're going to the cops?"

"No," he says sharply, the air around them thickening like tar. "I'd never do that. But I fucked up pretty bad."

"Just tell me," she says.

"I've been running drugs for a mobster. It was only supposed to be a couple jobs at first," he stops for a minute, tapping his fingers on the steering wheel, thinking it over. "The money, it was enough to actually, hell, I don't know, buy a house, a family-type car, maybe even pay for private school if I have kids."

She stares at him, watching his face as he tells his idealistic reality. She can't exactly place why Jordie actually thought his plan made any sense.

"You mean, like your stepfather, the one who hit you and drove your mother to prescription after prescription?" she asks, pretty fed up. "Money doesn't fix your problems."

He turns his head from the road for a split second, and she catches something—desperation, anger, frustration? She's not so sure.

"Kinda hard to believe that coming from the girl who has more money than problems," he says.

She rolls her eyes. "Yeah, because my life has been perfect. I saw my father a couple of months per year, and my mother was always pushing me into something—cheer-leading, ballet—I was pretty much her living, breathing, porcelain doll," she shakes her head, her hands moving too. "Give me a break."

"It doesn't matter why I did it," he says, slapping his hands on the wheel. "I did, and the point is, I fucked up."

"And why did you do all this?" she asks. "For Brooke?"

He slams on the brakes to the car. Everything shakes, but she barely jerks forward, her seatbelt still tightly fastened.

"Yes, I chose her," he says. "But you should be glad I chose her. Relieved you don't have to be on the sidelines for this."

"What exactly is this?" she asks.

No cars are behind them; they're still stopped in the middle of the street. The area is quiet enough, nothing but a few streetlamps and desolate buildings.

"I lost a car," he says.

"So, what, that's like $40,000? 100 max?" she says. "Big deal. It's a car. They sell more of them. You're a street racer.

Convince some idiot kid to race you for pink slips."

"This isn't a movie," he snaps. "And the car had $200,000 worth of cocaine in it."

"Are you fucking insane?" she screams.

He's screwed.

A fucking idiot too.

He shrugs his shoulders. "Probably, yeah."

But, she's right in a way, because this did involve drugs—just a lot more drugs than she'd thought. Hell, she kinda wishes he was on drugs now.

"And how are you going to get out of this?"

He shrugs his shoulders again. Infuriating.

"Do you have a plan?" she says, her voice frantic. "Wait a minute—does Brooke know?"

"I don't know what she knows, but I think she knows something."

"Wait, you didn't tell her?"

Fuck, she hates the girl, but this, this is too much.

"Won't the mob use her against you?"

He shakes his head. "I don't think so. Jared and her dad knew each other. He's bailed her out before."

"So, you know him because of her?" she asks.

He nods.

"And you've known him since?"

"The night she and I got together."

His hands are resting in his lap.

"So, he has something on you?"

He nods again.

"And now you're not very useful."

Another nod.

"What are you going to do?"

He raises his hand, turning the key in the engine, and pressing the gas. He drives kind of slow at first, like he's not quite sure where he's going.

Quietly he says, "I'll think of something."

Chapter 37: Brooke

She's sitting facing Jared, legs crossed, lest he get the idea that she would be a repeat offender. Perhaps she was willing to cheat on Jordie once to save him, or in a twisted anger plot, but it was a moment of weakness. She's determined it won't happen again.

Jared doesn't look too concerned. He's not emotional about anything, pretty much. This isn't a special occurrence for him.

It's not his life that hangs in the balance. What he has to lose is the currency of respect as well as real currency—like the money that Jordie had tossed away with the car.

"It should be no surprise that Jordie is in the crosshairs of the cops," he says to Brooke. "Not great."

She nods.

No, not great.

"What are you going to do?" she asks. She flicks her

fingers on her jeans.

He shakes his head, almost laughing. "Me?"

"Yes?" she asks.

He shrugs then folds his hands together. "Not my boy-friend; I don't want to save him."

"What does that mean?" she asks.

"You're the one who wants Jordie safe," he says. He stands, walks around his office, and pours two drinks of scotch. He brings her one and places it in her hands. "So, what are you willing to do?"

She swirls the scotch in her lap, not wanting to think about what exactly Jared's offer might entail. He has seen her through the darkest periods of her life, and even still, she knows better than to trust him.

But, without Jordie, what is she even fighting for? He may be ridiculous, but he's her anchor.

"Anything," she says. "The same he'd do for me."

Jared sips his drink, seems to think for a minute, and puts it down on a table. "Okay," he says.

"So, what do you want me to do?"

"Well, there's a cop that's been lurking at the races," he says. "One of my boys recognizes him."

Her face goes cold, stiff.

"Do you want me to…"

He shakes his head, laughing at her before he speaks. "No, but it's good to see that you'd go there."

"It's not my preference," she says.

He bobs his head. "Yeah, sure."

"So, then what?"

"We need to give him a better, more plausible story. Iron-clad. Something that doesn't just exonerate Jordie but benefits me more than getting rid of him does."

"And what would that be?"

"I want to expand," he says. "In order to do that, my brother needs to be out of focus —needs to be distracted."

"Distracted by what?"

"An eye for an eye. The cops need somebody, and I'm more than willing to hand Jordie over. It's not like I ever told him enough to sink me. His only leverage is over you and that night," he says.

"And if I do this, is Jordie free?"

"Maybe. That depends on how much he actually told the cop."

"So, what you're saying is that even if I do this, you're not going to guarantee anything?"

He walks forward, stands above her, and leers down at her.

"Brooke, I'm not asking," he says. "Do you think the cop isn't going to use the girlfriend angle? You're as good as locked up."

"Is that a threat?" she asks.

He shakes his head, sighs, then says, "No, but if you think I'm going to take the blame for your dead father, you're obviously demented."

Her demons are aligned like dominoes. The weight of her choice is finally pushing against her. "So, did you only help me in case you needed something some day?"

"That's how these kinds of deals work," he says. "What?

Did you think I did it out of the kindness of my heart?"

Her weight shifts. "I just didn't…"

"Didn't what?"

She swallows her breath before speaking. "It doesn't matter. Who are we going to pin this on?"

Chapter 38: Natalie

"I've been working a lot more lately," Ben says as he hands her an iced latte. Her favorite. Damn the boy, he always knows her best, even if she wants to let him go.

"I don't know if you can call what you're doing work," she says, taking the drink and having a sip.

He shrugs, "It pays. Besides, I start law school in September. Say what you want about Edge, but he looks out for me."

She curls her fingers around the cup, focusing on her red nail polish so that she doesn't look Ben in the face because she's trying to cut back on the addiction.

"Didn't he threaten you like a week ago?" she asks.

He nods. "Yeah, but he was stressed out. It's hard for him to know who he can trust."

"And out of all the people, he's going to trust you?" she asks, but it was probably too harsh because she can see Ben wince from the corner of her eye, so she quickly follows with, "Sorry."

He breathes through his nose, huffing, and stands from the bench in their usual spot. They meet there at least once a week, always to talk. Even if they're on the outs, even when she's successfully convinced herself that she hates him and that all of her problems are his fault, she still meets him.

In the winter when they meet, he brings hot chocolate or French vanilla lattes instead of iced coffee, but it's always the way she likes it, no matter the flavor. Maybe he's trying to win her heart back with coffee, but it's never going to be enough.

"I don't know why you hate me so much," he says standing before her, treading the thin line between emotional and angry. "I wanted everything with you."

She stands too, ready to walk away for him for the millionth time, but he places his hands on her shoulders, leans in, wraps her in a hug that she doesn't want, and whispers in her ear, "I love you."

She pushes him off, scowling at his words. "I don't love you," she says, feeling the words stinging on her tongue, like sucking on the end of a battery.

He lets his hands fall from her shoulders, "I don't believe you," he says.

"It doesn't matter if you believe me. It's the truth," she replies.

He shakes his head and sighs but doesn't speak.

"Why don't you understand that I don't love you?" she

asks, almost in tears. He has to understand that she can't love him. That he reminds her of everything she's lost and everything she never wanted to have.

"Because you keep showing up every week. No matter what. It's been a year, and you keep showing up," he says. "And without these weekly meetings, I feel like I'll jettison."

"I feel like that too," she says, her body shaking. She lets him wrap his arms around her, pulling her close as tears well up in her eyes.

"It's been a year today," he says, "And I still think of it every day."

She swallows her breath. Fresh, hot tears start to fall and stain Ben's white t-shirt as she cries against him. His grip tightens, holding her. After a few moments, she feels the trickling of moisture down her neck, his own tears falling down his face onto her body.

"I know we lost her," he says, "But I lost you too."

She tightens her grip on him. A year, or even ten, aren't going to be enough to make her forget. Her guilt, her pain, it all mixes together, and her tears fall harder. She gasps for breath, practically clawing Ben as she hugs his shirt.

"I never wanted a baby," she says, still crying, speaking despite the messy phlegm balling in her nose, "but this is killing me."

"I know," he says, patting her back, holding her close to him like she's the most cherished thing in the world to him.

"It's my fault we lost her," she says. "I didn't want her, so it was punishment."

She can hear him sigh, feeling his hand move as he wipes his own tears. "It's nobody's fault," he says, but she's pretty sure that's a lie.

She could never be with him. How do you build a life and a family with somebody after the first attempt burned down in flames?

Still, she lets Ben hold her. Without him today, she'd never keep going. She doesn't always think of her miscarriage, but when she does, the hopelessness takes her over, guts her of all other feeling besides pain.

"I'll leave for you," he says.

She bites her lip and pulls back from his shoulder. "What do you mean?" she asks.

"My job," he says, sounding very certain.

"And do you think Edge would just let you leave?" she asks.

He shakes his head and says, "I'm not sure, but if you ask me to, I will."

She nods, not sure of her answer.

"Think it through," he says. "Please."

"Okay," she says.

Chapter 39: Jordie

He had offered to take Amanda home; he hadn't quite expected her to literally be living in a garage. Maybe a house with a garage, but this is an actual automobile repair shop with a small apartment above.

A far cry from the practical mansion he had taken her home to as a teenager. The house where he felt the pressing weight of glass chandeliers and furniture that his mother would have salivated over, like something from her soap operas. But this place is tiny, grimy, and filled with dust. Even though Amanda has put out a few decorations and carved a tiny habitable space with a pink duvet on the cheap futon, it's still not the kind of place he'd expected of her.

"This is nice," he says as he continues to take in the room.

"No it's not," she says, placing her purse on the pale green countertop, "but it's private."

"It's a little… unexpected," he says.

She nods, not even making it a game to pretend like this is some sort of life choice that was clear from the get-go.

"My dad stopped having tenants when the shop went out of business. I don't think he even remembers he owns it," she says. "Plus, it's driving season for him, so he's not even in the city."

He sits on the futon which is still made into a bed. He's not sure if Amanda is going to snap at him, but she doesn't, and instead, she sits beside him. She looks tired, the underneath of her eyes darker than he remembers.

"Are you sleeping okay?" he asks even though he probably shouldn't be asking her these questions.

"No," she says truthfully, "I'm not."

"Me neither," he says, sighing between sentences. "Not since all this crap happened."

Amanda is picking at her chipped nail polish and says, "I still don't understand how this even happened."

He's not entirely sure himself. Smugness? Stupidity? A mixture of both? It's not like he *planned* for this to happen. "I don't know," he says.

Amanda watches him closely with her blue eyes, and he feels the guilt even more deeply. For some reason, even after all this time, her watching him with disappointment makes him sick to his stomach.

She presses her fingers to her mouth for a moment, then moves her hand to her chin. "Jordie, have you considered that part of you might have done this *accidentally on purpose?*" she asks.

"What?" he replies.

She moves her hands again, holding them together as she speaks, "You didn't want to be involved with Jared, so maybe part of you tanked the job because you knew it meant a change. For better or worse."

He stares at her, unable to process his thoughts clearly. He'd never do something like that. It would be stupid— even for him.

Yet, he's not so sure. Did he?

"That'd be crazy," he says.

She nods, still watching him with her blue eyes. "It would be."

He cups his head in his hands, pretty much ready to scream. He doesn't, though, which takes all the mental energy he has right now, keeping himself calm enough that he doesn't jump out of his skin.

He's not sure why it's easier to talk about this with Amanda even though he can feel the weight of her judgment pressing in on him. Maybe it's because Brooke's moral compass is a bit smudged and dirty. Or maybe he's just fucked up so much with Amanda that he surely can't disappoint her any more than he already has.

"Did I ever say sorry for what happened with Brooke?" he asks. Suddenly he needs to know, needs to be sure that what happened is clear to her—that he didn't do it to hurt her.

She shakes her head and says, "No."

"Well, I am," he says, dropping his hands to his side. "I'm sorry."

She purses her lips.

"Really, I am," he says, more worried by her silence than anything she could say. It's not like Amanda has ever been quiet.

Her nostrils flare, but a small smile comes across the crease of her lips.

"Thanks," she says, "But it doesn't matter anymore."

"Yeah, I guess," he says. He has thought about it, though. It's not like he didn't love her too, he just got so swept up in his feelings for Brooke that he couldn't untie himself.

"I'm more concerned about the mob boss and the cop vying for your life," she says. "What are you going to do about it?"

He's been asking himself the same question since it happened. He's even been avoiding Brooke because he knew she'd ask the same question or even stab him to solve the problem for him. He's no closer to finding an answer than he was the day after it happened.

His hands feel like they've been washed in acid, trembling slightly. Before this, he'd seldom experienced anxiousness. Now he can't stop himself from shaking whenever he thinks about it.

"I honestly don't know," he says, holding his hands together to stop the rattling. "I don't think there's anything I can do."

She shakes her head, her lip trembling. "So, what, you're just going to give up?" she asks.

"I didn't say that; I just don't know what I can do. It's not like I'm smarter than either of them."

"That's probably true," she says.

He had at least expected her to put up some fight to that statement, but nope, she knows, like everybody else does, that he's hopeless. It's not like his stupidity has escaped him. Time after time he's made the wrong fucking choice.

"I missed you," he says, fully aware of the short distance between them on the futon.

He watches as she swallows her breath, tilting her head away from him so that he can hardly see her eyes. He forgot, somehow, just how bright a blue they were.

If Brooke knew he was even considering the way Amanda's blue eyes compared to her green, she'd probably choke him to death.

Whatever; it's not like he's not going to die anyways. Better it come from somebody who loves him than somebody else.

"I missed you too," she says, her head turning back so that he can see her full face again. "For a while."

"Just a while?" he asks.

"I wasn't going to miss you forever," she says, scowling.

"Sorry," he says. "I didn't mean to hit a nerve."

She shakes her head and says, "It's fine."

It's hard to admit to himself, but he's wondering why he ever chose Brooke instead of Amanda. Not that he deserved to be the one to have the choice between them. He's just not sure why, in the scheme of things, he'd felt so strongly for Brooke. Maybe if he had never helped her—if her father wasn't a part of things. Maybe his entire life would be different now. And maybe he and Amanda would still be together.

He feels the distance between them, how close and yet how far away they are. He leans toward her, closing the tiny gap and placing his hand on the side of her head. He pushes strands of blonde hair from the front of her face with his thumb.

"Your hair is shorter than it was," he says. It used to go down to her chest, now it stops just under her neck.

"I cut it when I stopped cheerleading. I needed a change," she says.

"You're beautiful," he says, leaning in closer, finally feeling as though he's found his way back to safety.

Amanda's eyes are wide, watching him, not saying anything as he moves closer.

He takes a risk and moves closer, kissing her lips, wanting to taste the world and life that he left behind.

As he kisses her, for a brief moment it feels as though she's kissing back, like her weight is ready to press against his. Maybe he could leave behind the life he tore apart with Brooke and start over the way it should have been. Maybe…

Amanda's hand pushes against his chest, pushing him off her. "Jordie, stop it," she says, her breath heavy.

"I'm sorry," he says, not quite sure what came over him. "I just— "

"I don't care," she says, moving so that there's a greater distance between them than there was before. "I'm not Brooke, and I'm not you."

"What do you mean?" he asks.

"I'm not going to kiss a guy with a girlfriend. Like I said, I'm not Brooke."

He bites his lip. She's certainly called him out on his bullshit. He just felt so good next to her, so normal.

"I didn't mean to," he says.

"Cut the crap, Jordie," Amanda says, now standing. "You always do what you want."

"I'm losing it," he says. "I'm terrified."

Amanda kneels down before him, her eyes first fixed on his expression and then lowering to his hands that are trembling once more.

She takes his hands into her own, shakes her head, and says, "Jordie, we'll find a way, okay? I'm not going to let you die."

"I'm not your problem," he says truthfully. He's not even sure that he should be Brooke's problem either. His latest bad choice might well be his last.

"This isn't about being my problem. I may not want to date you, but that doesn't mean I want you dead," she says, running her fingers through his and holding his hand tighter. "We'll figure this out."

Chapter 40: Brooke

She has been waiting for the guilt to catch up with her. The price she had paid for giving in to Jared's offer was supposed to be a tarnished conscience. She was supposed to spend her days and nights holed up in bed, a pit in her stomach so large it could sprout a tree.

The only unsettling feeling she has is that she doesn't feel guilty. She did what had to be done. Made a deal with the devil and kept going, waking up and falling asleep just as she had before.

Except now she's angrier at Jordie.

Because of him, she now has to settle his score—keep him alive, fix the mess he's made.

Jared had tasked her with solving a riddle: How does a cop get a car full of drugs and no driver?

It's becoming clear that the answer to the riddle involves an act of complete stupidity. What that act is, she's not sure.

See, even if Jared wants to let Jordie go, wants to fix this mess, move on, and go about their business, he can't.

Not while Jordie's lips are sealed and loose ends are fraying like strings just waiting to be pulled, ready to unravel and tear the entire tapestry.

Whatever Jordie is hiding, he's making it worse. Can't clean up a mess if you don't know where the spill is.

She's pulled apart everything in their apartment. Drawers, coats, jean pockets. His laptop hasn't offered any clues either.

So, she'll have to tell him she knows.

How she knows too.

Or maybe she can get around it. Keep that monster in Pandora's box.

But she's made her bed, and she'll have to lie in it. Fair enough.

Depending on his answer, she may not be able to keep protecting him. Keep leveraging whatever history her and Jared have to keep him above ground. She's running out of history, though.

Jared may have known her father, but he also hated her father.

He may have slept with her a few times, but guys like him can get sex without blinking.

Not only is he hot, he's top of the pyramid.

He's going to get bored of her sooner rather than later.

Losing Jordie is the last thing in the world she wants.

But what will she do if he doesn't come clean?

Or, what will she do if he does come clean, and his

answers are something she can't live with.

Her phone rings, and she answers. Jared is on the other line.

"Have you found anything," he asks?

"I haven't," she says, holding the phone to her face as she uses her other hand to keep looking.

"At least he's smart enough not to leave evidence around," Jared says. "There's hope for that idiot yet."

"I'm not sure what I'm looking for," she says.

"I don't know, anything from that night."

"Okay, fine," she says, hissing as she speaks.

She's agreed to go along with Jared's plan, but that doesn't mean that she's enthusiastic.

Jordie's the type of guy that doesn't have a lock on his phone. She's lucky if he locks the door when he goes out. Absent-minded, never thinking about the consequences. Which is why she's so worried.

What kind of shit have you gotten into? she thinks.

The door to the apartment opens. "Bye," she says quickly and clicks off her phone, slapping it onto the table and going for the fridge to open it and pretend she's simply preparing food.

"Hey," Jordie says as he walks in, placing his keys on the table next to the phone. "Were you talking to somebody?"

"Yeah, just a friend," she says.

"Ah," he says. "Whatcha making?"

"Um," she has to think about it a little too long. "Not sure, there's not much in here."

She closes the refrigerator.

"Oh," he says. He walks across the room and pulls her into a hug. "Maybe we could go out to eat?"

"Yeah," she says, barely returning the affection.

"What's wrong?" he asks, pulling back.

Well, Jordie, she thinks, you're a fucking idiot, and now I have to contend with the mafia that may or may not want to kill you.

"Nothing," she says, but she's not trying to be convincing. She's still pissed off he's gotten her into this mess, and her snooping uncovered nothing useful.

Chapter 41: Axel

When a petite blonde showed up at his motel room door, he wasn't so sure he should let her in. She couldn't be much older than 23. He sees her through the tiny hole on the door. He's only been back for twenty minutes, and he has no idea who she is.

But she keeps banging on the door despite his ignoring her.

"Hello?" she says, and rather loudly adds, "You're the cop, right?"

He flings the door open, grabs her arm, and pulls her inside the room, slamming the door shut as quickly as he had opened it.

"Ow," she says, rubbing her arm where he'd grabbed her. "What was that for?"

"Because you were shouting that I'm a cop," he hisses.

Her head tilts to the side, looking him over, and says,

"And you're not?"

He walks to the room's mini-fridge and pulls out a beer. Pretty sure this conversation is going to require alcohol.

"Why do you want to know?" he asks, offering her a beer.

Thankfully, he'd picked up his dirty clothes and tossed them in the bathroom that morning. Not that it should matter.

She shakes her head saying, "No thanks, I'm driving," and she invites herself to sit on the bed, still watching him.

He nods. "You still haven't said why you're asking. Actually," he pauses for a moment and scrunches his face up, "how did you even get here?"

"I followed you," she says as though it's not a big deal, and crosses her legs, still perched on his bed.

"You what?" he asks.

Great, his cover is so *unbelievably* unbreakable that he was discovered and tailed by a 5'2 blonde wearing high-heeled boots.

"I saw you at the race," she says.

"Yeah, I got that part," he says, mulling over what this means for a second before speaking. "Still not sure on the *why*."

She stands from the bed, walking through the room and eyeing his files. He walks in front of the desk, blocking them from her view.

"I'm here because of Jordie," she says.

He now recognizes her as the blonde that was fighting with Jordie's girlfriend, Brooke, at the race. "What, are you his *second* girlfriend?"

Her wistfulness fades away, her expression going blank. "No, but I was once. That's not the point," she says hastily.

Cover blown, he brings his hands to his forehead, rubbing his fingers along his temples. He's not surprised that Jordie told somebody, but to be honest, he wasn't expecting this particular bombshell in the shape of Britney Spears.

"I'm not *a cop*," he says, placing his beer, untouched, on the table near his files.

"Okay," she says, her voice now a little shaky. She clearly doesn't believe him. He can also tell she's frustrated, even a little worried.

"You came here because of Jordie?" he asks and then adds, "Why?"

He's put together that Jordie's told her some, if not all, of the story, but he wants to hear it from her. Wants her to trust him, or at the very least show her motivations. Anything that points out why she's followed him here to his not-so-hidden hideaway. Yep, time to bail on this place.

She's pacing his motel room, three silver bangle bracelets clinking together as she walks. "He told me about the car with the drugs, and there's this guy who wants to kill him as well as a cop that's after him," she barely breathes between words but finds the time to add, "I thought you were *that cop*."

"I'm not a cop," he says again, then moves his hands from his face to cross them over his chest. "I'm Agent Wariloe"

"Agent?" she asks. "What are you, a spy?"

"What?" He shakes his head, a little frustrated but also

bewildered. "No, I'm FBI. Why would you think I'm a spy?"

Her hands are up in the air, aghast. "I don't know, I don't, I just… I'm still rattled by all of this. That Jordie…"

"Is an idiot?" He probably shouldn't have said it, especially with her clear state of panic, but honestly, Jordie's propensity for fucking up never ceases to amaze him. "He shouldn't have told you anything," Axel says with a sigh.

The girl has tears in her eyes, and her state of panic seems to be increasing. "I can't believe I stalked a federal agent. Is that a crime?" she says in the middle of gasping breaths.

His first and only instinct, Jordie nonsense aside, is to calm her down.

"I think we can let this go," he says, placing his hands on her shoulders. "Here, look at me."

She's still gasping, her panic attack not letting up.

"What's your name?" he asks.

Through quick breaths, she replies, "Amanda."

"Okay, Amanda," he says, "I want you to count with me… 1, 2, 3, 4…"

She repeats him, her breaths becoming slower with each number. By the time they reach 10, her breath is normal, and the only tears left are the ones staining her face. Her eyeliner and mascara have run down her cheeks.

He helps her to the bed, sitting her back down.

"I'm sorry," she says as he walks to the fridge, retrieving a bottle of water and bringing it to her, handing it over.

"Don't be, but you should drink."

She obliges, a far cry from the determined force that

banged on his door just a few minutes before.

He sits in a flower-patterned armchair in the corner of the room facing her and waits for her to have several gulps of water before he speaks. "So, Amanda, why exactly did you come to me? You said it yourself; I want to arrest Jordie."

"I don't know," she says, her voice still shaky and a bit hoarse from hyperventilating. "I thought maybe you'd help."

He raises his thumb to his teeth, chewing on the nail for a moment. Thinking over the possible scenarios in his head. He doesn't have any leads, and he obviously needs to ensure that Amanda doesn't run around telling his secrets. But what could she offer, and more importantly, why would she?

"Help you how?" he asks her.

"I can't lose Jordie," is all she says.

Chapter 42: Jordie

He can't think clearly. His muscles are tense; his head is fuzzy and blurry. He can't even remember the difference between the two. He's jumping through hoops in his mind. From what he can figure, no matter what he does or what decision he makes next, he's cornered. The mouse just underneath the cat's claw. He's starting to think that he's not going to survive this. 24 is too young to die, but he's probably going to because he's incapable of making good decisions.

Maybe it's karma—for helping Brooke, for choosing her. For choosing death, destruction, and crime over somebody as sweet as her. Or maybe it's just dumb luck. Nothing to do with fate—just what happens when a string of bad decisions come together and chokes at your neck like a noose. What if Jared comes after him? If he's already planning his death? What if it's all going to end? Or what if he does something to Brooke? Amanda? What if he knows all of his secrets, and he's just waiting for the opportune moment to pounce? Maybe he could go to Axel and cut a deal, tell him something about Jared that's useful. Then, though, he would be signing his own death warrant.

The worst part isn't knowing that he's fucked up or knowing that either Axel or Jared could be the end of him. The worst part is not knowing when it's going to catch up with him or who will be the one to finally pull the trigger.

He's pacing his apartment. His blood is boiling. His heart is racing. He walks to the counter, takes a hit off a bong, and paces some more. Drugs are the last thing he should be doing. It's not like they were hard to find though; he just had to ask one of Jared's guys and cough up enough cash. He thought it would help him think. Instead, he's blurring out faster. The room is spinning out of control.

The THC is doing nothing for his panic attack, just making him unable to focus on the little details that are pressing against the weight of his body. Just making it so that he can't think of *how* to fix it. He can only think of the *why* he's freaking out.

Over and over on a loop.

He, Axel, and the dance over one car filled with fine white powder.

The job he never wanted. For the man he never wanted to meet.

For the girl that he's not sure is worth it.

He wonders whether if he does go to the cops—if they'll take a plea and whisk him to a safe house. He wonders if they protect people if he claims that he was bewitched. Mesmerised and wrapped around the claws of a woman, a she-devil. The kind of girl who kills her father and walks away like it never happened.

He thinks he's hallucinating when he sees her in front of him, walking toward him.

"Jordie," she says, "Are you okay?"

Her image distorts. He can almost see her devil horns peeking out. The demon that he chose to love, that he still loves. The woman that he gave it up for. That he'd give it up for again. *What have I given up though?* he wonders. He has to really focus on the life he had before Brooke. There was Amanda and his car. There was a mother who barely wanted him. The stepfather who hit him. There was a boy who raced because he *was good*, because when the people watched him, they didn't pity him. He wasn't the kid that ruined their figure, the resentful feature at the dinner table. Nope, he was liked. Wanted there.

"You ruined my life!" he yells at the image of Brooke. The figment of his imagination that haunts his waking dreams.

"I… what?" Brooke asks, examining his face. The figure trying to get inside his head and torture him. Maybe she'll shoot him like she did her father. Put him out of his misery.

"You ruined my life when I chose to save you," he says.

"You saved me from what?" she asks, placing her hands on his shoulders, trying to steady him. Her touch feels so close, so heavy, so real for a vision.

"I don't know," he says, his entire body shaking. His heartbeat becoming so loud that it's all he can hear. "I fucked up."

"Sit down, Jordie," she says, guiding him to their cracked black leather sofa.

He follows her, shaking out of his trance enough to realize that she's really there.

"I kissed Amanda," he says, blurting it out. "I'm sorry…"

Brooke shakes her head, but she doesn't seem ready to cry or even kill him. Maybe she's fallen out of love with him. He should be relieved. Instead, he's terrified. He realizes what he's done, why he did everything for her. Every moment leading to this one. That night he came to get her from her father's, watching the fear in her eyes as she stood above her father—the panic, the torrential heaviness of what had transpired. And he remembers holding her that night as she cried, as he told her that Aaron had deserved what he got, as he kissed the pale yellow bruises across her skin, the only living remnants of Aaron to be found.

She just watches him, sits beside him, and presses her hand to his face. "It's okay," she says and then kisses his cheek. "I love you."

"You do?" he asks.

She presses her nose to his, lips still close to his cheek. "I do, and there's something you should know too."

"What?" he asks as her face pulls out so that she can look him in the eye.

Her green eyes are shining underneath the white light, and he regrets ever thinking that Amanda's eyes could be prettier. Atop of his anxiety, he feels guilt that he ever could think that Brooke isn't worth all of the pain.

Because he'd do it all again. The worst of it. *Anything* for her.

"I slept with Jared," she says.

He pulls away from her, pushes her just slightly so that he can get up. All of the fog from his brain lifts and is instead replaced by lightning. "You what?" he says, almost screaming.

Brooke stands, her body tense as she watches him. "I thought it would buy you more time."

"And how did you think *having sex* with the man who wants to *kill me* was going to help?" he demands.

"Well, we used to have a thing before you and me," she says. "There was a time he made me feel safe. I thought, maybe, part of him cared."

"Are you kidding me?" he demands. "Brooke, the *only* person that Jared cares about is himself. He's going to leverage your father's death over you the first chance he gets."

She turns away from him, and he sees tears starting to fall down her face as she says, "Yeah, he's made that threat."

He walks toward her and wipes her tears with his hands, pulling her to him, and kissing her forehead. "We'll fix this," he says.

She laughs, very solemnly, then says, "No, we won't."

"It wasn't supposed to happen like this," he adds seriously, still high, but starting to crash.

Chapter 43: Natalie

Admitting out loud that she's still upset over her miscarriage has rattled her. In a way, for the last year, she hasn't allowed herself to live her life because she's felt she hasn't deserved it. If she is so terrible that she felt some *relief* at not being a mother, then how does she deserve a chance at a future?

Of course, rationally she knows it wasn't her fault. There's no cosmic balance that self-corrects when you make a bad decision. If there were, Ben would probably have been smited long ago for turning to drug dealing to handle his own emotional trauma. The two of them are quite the pair. She's sitting at the desk in her room, filling out a paper that she had printed from her computer. It turned out that the paper she had ripped up the other morning in a vodka-fueled hate session was purely symbolic. The website for her choice engineering program had told her she had another two weeks to fill out her form. So, she fills in her answers on the sheet, and she wonders how she's going to pay for school or what this means for her and Ben—if anything. The truth is, she finally feels like she can start to fix things and to build something again.

Even with so many unanswered questions, she knows that things will be alright because at least she's starting to ask them. Instead of hiding and punishing herself for the life that could have had, she's ready to start something new for herself.

Ryder knocks on her half open door.

"Come in," she says.

"What's that?" he asks, mildly curious and holding a plate of leftover rice that he hands to her.

She accepts the plate and says, "Thank you," then looks down at the paper. "It's my application," she says.

"It is?" he asks.

She smiles and sets the plate down next to the application.

"Yeah, I think I'll apply and see how it goes. I'm not really doing much else right now."

Ryder nods, and he doesn't say anything about it, but she catches him smiling in the corner of his mouth.

"Thanks for the food," she says, "It looks good."

"You're welcome," he says.

"So, how are things with you and Amanda?" she asks, wanting to change the topic away from school because if she talks too much about it, she'll rip up this page too.

"What do you mean?" he asks, walking further into the

room and sitting on the bed for a second.

"I don't know, you two seem closer lately," she says, turning her swivel chair to face him. "Like, you haven't even complained about her in a week."

"Yeah, I guess," he says.

She laughs and says, "You're totally into her."

"Stop it," he says, but his voice is still playful, not completely pissed off.

"Maybe you two should race each other; that's always worked for me and…" She stops herself. "You know who."

"You can say his name; he's not Voldemort," Ryder says.

"With the way you've talked about him in the past, he may as well be," Natalie says.

Ryder shrugs. "I don't know what you see in him, but by the way you two have been eyeing each other, it's obvious that it's not over."

"You noticed?" she asks, surprised.

"Hard not to," he says. "You keep running off with him to dark alleys."

She bites her lip and then shakes her head and says, "I honestly don't know what I'm doing there."

Ryder stands again, walking toward the door. "Well, maybe you should figure it out."

"Probably," she says, "but I'm not sure if I'm going to like the answer."

"Just do what makes you happy," he says. "Why is it so complicated?"

"You *know* why," she says.

He inhales, and then his face turns solemn. "I know, but

neither of you are the same people you were a year ago. Consider your options with Ben now and not the Ben that he was."

"So, consider whether or not I want to have a future with a dime-store criminal instead of the potential high-rate lawyer?" she asks.

Ryder nods. "I didn't say you should get back together. I'm saying you need to decide what you want in life."

"You're confusing," she says.

"No more than you," he replies.

She thanks him once more for the food, and he leaves the room, closing the door behind him. She considers what Ben had said—that he would be willing to find a way out of the mafia for her. She wonders if that's even possible, and she wonders how the two of them could get by. Him in law school, and her an engineering student. The student loans alone might be enough to destroy the plan. But they'd be together, and they'd be the people that they always wanted to be, save for a few broken pieces.

She places her palms on her face, trying to deliberate. There's still a part of her, though that part of her is growing smaller, that wonders if happiness is possible.

Chapter 44: Brooke

A rasping knock on her door takes her by surprise. The knocking continues, and her heart jumps. Jordie isn't home, but it's not like he'd knock, and her first instinct is that it's the cops, or worse, it's Jared.

No matter who it is, she has a sinking feeling that whoever is at the door is going to either put her in a body bag or handcuffs.

She rises from her chair slowly, even takes the time to push it into the table—something she never does. Anything to make the walk to the door slower. On the way, she rearranges magazines on the counter as though appearances are going to matter.

She reaches the door and slowly opens it. Her heart thumps louder as she swings it open, revealing the face on the other side of the door.

She figures she's finally lost her mind and gone full on

psycho because there he is…

The man she murdered 4 years ago.

Aaron smirks at her, "Thought you killed me, did you?" he says as he enters, closing the door behind him. "Tough luck, kiddo."

"I know I killed you," she says, voice shaking. "I saw you bleeding on the floor."

He nods and takes a seat at the table. "You did, that's true."

"You were dead," she says, "You're dead."

All she can see is shades of red, her vision coming in and out as she tries to decipher his face.

He raises his shirt to show a healed wound, now a scar. "You didn't hit anything vital, unfortunately for you," he says.

She backs up, standing against the counter. Whatever sick game this is, she's sure she won't win. If Aaron truly is alive, that means the man she *tried* to murder is a walking, talking, and *breathing* man with a grudge.

"But Jared's men, they took your body," she says. "I… We… Jordie and I, we saw them take your body…"

"You saw *men* take me. Trouble is I wasn't dead, and those men weren't Jared's. At least not in the way he thinks they were," Aaron says.

A wash of emotions overtakes her, and she tries to steady her breathing. She feels oddly relieved, yet she also feels completely disenfranchised. The last four years of her life, both good and bad, have been influenced by that night. Still, it doesn't change *why* she shot him in the first place.

"What kind of daughter shoots her own father?" Aaron asks. His eyes are narrowed, but his face is almost in a grin, like he's testing her.

Her body is numb. The kind of daughter that shoots her own father, of course, is the kind that wanted him to die.

"I…" she tries to say, but she can't find the rest of her sentence. Seeing Aaron here is too… jarring.

Before she can continue, the apartment door opens and Jordie walks in. He doesn't close the door, he just stares at the table, completely dumbfounded.

"Is that…?

The first time Jordie had met Aaron, he was *presumed* dead on the floor of her childhood home. The night that they had forged a bond over the unspeakable act she had committed—when both of them had tied themselves to Jared, for better or worse.

She nods as though she needs to affirm his question.

"Does Jared know you're alive?" Jordie asks.

Aaron laughs. "How stupid do you think I am?"

She doesn't answer, and neither does Jordie. Pretty stupid, apparently.

"You may not have killed me," he says, "but Jared was more than willing to dump my still alive body in a river."

Jared had given her the gun. Jared had convinced her that her father was dangerous. Jared, it seems, had been egging her on from the start. Letting the dishevelled daughter take care of her father. Yeah, Aaron *was* abusive, but she was ready to leave. If she hadn't had a gun…

"He played me," she says, nearly losing her balance, but

Jordie whips forward to steady her, holding her up by the waist. "That fucking bastard."

"Why, though?" Jordie asks Aaron. "Why did Jared go through all that trouble?"

Aaron crosses his arms on his chest and says, "He doesn't take betrayal lightly, I guess."

"You betrayed Jared?" Jordie asks, honestly sounding a little impressed, hopeful even. Like he hadn't thought of it as an option.

She almost reaches up and smacks him to remind him that Aaron nearly ended up dead for his indiscretion, but she's too fatigued to move.

"I did," Aaron says, arms still crossed. "And I still am."

Chapter 45: Amanda

Amanda and Ryder are sitting on her WRX, chatting normally. Talking about the car and the latest parts. Having an informed discussion about how she can become a better driver. Everything is normal, executed without an inch of her unease showing on her face. At least she thinks so because Ryder hasn't said anything.

Axel had told her to act normal. To go about her day and do everything she would normally. After she had straight up stalked a federal agent, it's probably best to listen to what he has to say.

He couldn't promise that Jordie would be safe, but he did tell her that he'd try.

She's not sure if she can trust him, but other than the mafia, who else could she go to? And, unlike Jordie, she's not going to marry herself to the mob and hope for the best.

Ryder asks her a question, but he looks annoyed.

"Huh?" she says, not having heard him.

He shakes his head, "It doesn't matter."

"I'm sorry. Just tell me what you said," she says.

"What's going on with you?" he asks.

She has to come up with something—a lie that covers her distraction.

Instead, she's half-saved because Jordie walks up and asks, "Amanda, can I talk to you?"

Ryder's teeth are showing. A reaction that seems to happen whenever he's close to Jordie.

Axel had told her to stay away from Jordie, that associating with him could put her in danger too, but the dark circles under his eyes are concerning.

Caught at a crossroads, she's not sure what to do. Ryder is practically snarling as Jordie awaits her answer.

"For a minute," she says reluctantly.

Ryder says nothing, just walks away toward his car. She's left facing Jordie who may or may not still be ready to climb over the edge.

"What do you want?" she asks, her voice colder than she wants it to be. Even if she wants to save Jordie, she needs to keep him at a distance, especially after he kissed her.

"I told Brooke about the kiss," he says.

She shakes her head and says, "Yeah, so?"

"I don't think she's mad," he says, "but things are getting crazier."

"Crazier how?" she asks. For whatever reason, Jordie has trusted her instead of anybody else around him.

Perhaps Axel was wrong, and she should talk to him. Let him tell her everything he's willing to, and then she can relay the information. Jordie might be too stupid to know when he's in too deep and when to finally talk to the cops, or FBI rather, but she's not.

"I don't know," he says. "Everybody is trying to use Brooke's past against me. Everything I do is for her, and she's going to drown me."

"Maybe it's time to let her go," she says, shifting her weight on her feet.

"I don't know," he says, shaking, "I love her."

She nods. "Okay, but what does this have to do with your situation?" she asks.

"She told me she slept with Jared," he says, "to try and buy me more time."

Amanda narrows her eyes. *Brooke and Jordie are clearly made for each other*, she mentally notes before continuing. "Wait, so she's trying to get you out of this?"

"Yeah," he says, "but Jared played her."

"Played her how?" she asks.

"He's using her past against us. Brooke…" He pauses, chews on his lip, and turns away from her. "Never mind, I'm going to go."

"What did Brooke do?" she asks. "It's not like there's anything that would surprise me. I already hate her."

He shakes his head. "No, that doesn't matter."

She shrugs, acting as she normally would.

"What does he have on her?" she asks again, thinking any information that she has can be used to give Axel an idea to save Jordie.

Jordie sighs but leans closer to her, practically whispering in her ear, "I was there the night that she killed her father,"

Amanda's mouth drops open, and she pulls back. "You were what?" she says a little too loudly. "Wait… she what?"

"It was the night we hooked up," he says, head hanging low. "Listen, Amanda, I'm so sorry… everything… it's such a mess."

It's not like she ever liked Brooke, but the thought that the first person she ever loved left her for a murderer… Her thoughts jumble, and she feels bile in her stomach rising, nearly about to throw up. "A mess? This is beyond a mess."

"You don't understand; he hit her," he says. As though that's a reason to flat out murder a person. "It was self-defence."

"And did you call the cops?" Amanda asks, her voice strained.

He shakes his head.

"I can't take this," she says, turning away from him and walking as fast as she can. "Don't follow me," she hisses.

Everything bad, it seems, leads back to Brooke. She wonders how Brooke could be so compelling that after killing her own father, Jordie would still choose her.

He doesn't listen and follows her.

Luckily for her, they walk straight into where Ryder is standing, talking to Natalie and Eric.

"Is there a problem?" Ryder asks. Natalie's eyes are wide, curious to see what's going on.

"Yes, there's a problem," Amanda says, voice crisp.

Jordie shakes his head and says, "No, there's not."

Ryder's stature changes—his shoulders are raised back, ready for whatever Jordie throws at him. "I think you should go," he says.

"This isn't any of your business," Jordie says.

She wants to push him in front of two of the cars ready to take off for a race. "Jordie, seriously, I can't do this, you need to go," she says, not sure if she'll even go back to Axel. Brooke and Jordie deserve each other. "In fact, breaking up with me was the best thing you ever did," she says.

Jordie's eyes go wide, like he's just been shot. "Amanda… let's just talk," he pleads.

Ryder steps forward, blocking Jordie. "You heard her; you should go."

She's not sure why Ryder is being protective, but she's thankful for his interference.

"So, you're with him now?" Jordie asks, grumbling, like he has any right to care.

"The only thing that matters is that I'm not with you," she says.

Ryder moves closer to her, his back straight, ready to drag Jordie away if he has to.

Jordie takes that as a confirmation of his bias, and instead of backing down, he growls, "Great, so you've just found *another* racer. It's clear you're just trying to replace me."

"Not everything is about you, Jordie," she says.

Ryder, having enough of the theatrics, moves forward. Amanda hadn't really realized before, but his muscles are rather pronounced, like he spends a great deal of time lifting weights. "Jordie, just take off; you've already made a fool of yourself."

Jordie spits on the ground but finally relents and turns to get in his GTO. She can faintly see him slam his hands on the wheel before he drives off.

Natalie is the first to speak, "What the fuck was that about?" she asks.

Ryder shrugs, finally relaxing. "Just Vodheo being Vodheo."

Chapter 46: Brooke

4 Years Ago

She sits on a gray sofa across from Jordie. Her entire body trembles and shakes. Her heart rate hasn't gone down in two hours. Her shirt has red blotches all over it with some blood still smeared on her arm.

"Maybe you should take a shower?" Jordie says. He's standing above her, holding a towel toward her. She hadn't noticed him leave or enter the room. Her thoughts are jumbling together as she tries to piece everything together. Should she feel guilty, or should she feel relieved?

She takes the towel slowly and tries to stand, her legs wobbling. Jordie holds out his arms, steading her from falling. She leans her head on his chest, pressing her eyes against his shoulder as hot tears stream out. The towel falls from her hands onto the floor.

Jordie hesitates for a moment, but his hands move to her

back and press her closer to him, wrapping his arms around her and squeezing.

"Come on," he says, pulling her back for a moment to lean down and pick up the towel. When he stands, he rearranges her under his left arm, holding her against him as he leads them both toward a small bathroom.

Once in the bathroom, Jordie's eyes scan Brooke. He hesitates for a moment.

She's unable to think of anything to say, lost adrift somewhere back in her childhood home where Jared's men are sopping up the remainder of her father's blood, disinfecting Aaron from the cheap vinyl flooring, erasing any proof of his existence.

Jordie turns the nozzle of the shower and adjusts the curtain.

He moves toward her, and all she can think is that she wants to lean on him again. Her arms move to wrap around him, but he stops her.

"Shower," he says, then his eyes move down to her shirt. At first, she assumes he's looking at her cleavage, but when she looks down, she sees the red splotches.

She nods at him, finally starting to regain some cognizance.

It dawns on her that Jordie is involved now too. Her father's blood joins the two of them in some twisted fate.

"I'm sorry," she says, holding back more tears. "You don't deserve to be involved in this."

Jordie shakes his head and then says, "I'm just glad that you're okay."

"I'm a murderer," she says, testing the words out loud. They slice her throat as she says them.

Jordie takes her hands in his and leans forward, his eyes focused only on hers.

"Murderers don't kill monsters," he says.

She knows that Jordie isn't hers, but after killing her own father, it's hard to consider the feelings of Jordie's bitchy, blonde girlfriend.

Brooke pulls back for a moment, pulling her tank top over her head, and leans down, turning on the shower nozzle.

Jordie becomes still, his expression blank; he seems to be trying not to watch her.

She slips out of her ripped skinny jeans and takes her bra and underwear off, letting them fall to the floor.

Jordie still hasn't moved. He's still catatonic—basically a statue.

She moves closer to him, her hands on his shirt, pulling from the bottom to take it off. Jordie helps her by pulling the rest off.

Within seconds, his pants are gone too.

What's one more sin to add to the list?

They fumble together to get into the shower, the blood washing off her arm, slipping down her naked leg, and finally swirling with the water and going down the drain.

Jordie's hands are on the back of her neck, his lips lunging toward hers as she grasps at his back, pulling him closer.

Chapter 47: Natalie

As she pulls her Chevelle into the parking lot where they're going to race that night, she feels lighter. She has made a decision about her and Ben, one that she's not sure he'll go for, but she hopes that he will.

They've spent too long worried about their past and about the gruesome details of what *could have been.* She'd finally decided, while mulling it over through 6 iced lattes, that enough was enough. She wants to move on with her life.

It was hard to hide the excitement in her voice when she called him, but she managed to hide it just enough that he seemed normal when she hung up.

It wasn't an easy realization to come to that she still loves him. But it was harder to deny with each passing day.

She parks her car and gets out, taking her time as she moves through the crowd to find Ben. It takes longer than she expects because he's off in the corner. She doesn't see

Amanda or Ryder. She's glad because it would be harder to do this with a larger audience.

"Ben," she says, trying to hide her smile.

"Yeah?" he asks, but he seems a little on edge, like he's waiting for something to go wrong.

"Do you still love me?" she asks.

His eyes widen, but he says, "You know that I do."

"I want to get back together," she says.

Instead of smiling like he should, his eyes grow wide, and he snarls at her, "Move."

"What?" she asks, turning around to look behind her, stepping in front of Ben at whatever he's facing. But the night lights up like fireworks, and she hears a burst of popping noises. Fireworks maybe? Cars backfiring? The second is more likely, but she suddenly feels dizzy.

Her face feels hot. It takes her several moments to understand the stinging feeling in her abdomen that has replaced her butterflies, and it takes her a few seconds too long to realize that the screaming she's hearing and the cars taking off have something to do with the reason she freefalls toward the ground.

Ben's strong arms prop her up against him, frantically saying her name, but she's having trouble hearing anything. It takes a moment, but she does put it together. Just not why.

"Ben?" she asks.

"Nat?" he says, half pleading with her.

"What happened?" she asks. "Was I shot?"

"Yeah," he says, then yells for somebody to call 911.

She feels the wetness go through her shirt, and as she looks down, she can see a pool of crimson.

"If you asked me again, I'd say yes," she says.

"What?" he asks, his voice still frantic, eyes searching the small crowd that has yet to get in their cars and flee.

"If you proposed again," she says, "I'd say yes."

She can see a tear falling from his eye, "I'll ask you when this is over," he says.

She sees Ryder come up beside Ben, Amanda next to him.

"Oh my god," she hears, but her ears are a little foggy, and it could have been Ryder or Amanda that said it.

"Natalie," Ryder says, holding her hand. "Stay awake."

She's trying to but failing.

She wants to tell Ryder about her plans, but she can't seem to find the words.

Her mind is softening around the edges, like the end of a movie where the scene begins to fade out. Slowly, surely, fading away.

"Natalie," she hears Amanda say. "Natalie, wake up."

But she's not sure that she can. Her eyes are fluttering. She can hear sirens coming, and she's worried that her friends will get arrested—but she also wants to know who did this.

"Who was the bullet for?" she asks, trying to find answers because she's sure that there's not a lot of time left to ask questions.

She sees Ryder swallow his breath, but Amanda answers for them. Ben is still holding her in his arms, keeping her propped up.

"It looks like for Ben," Amanda says.

"Why?" she asks.

"I'm not sure," Ben whispers, "But I'm so sorry."

She shakes her head and says, "I'm not. I couldn't lose you too."

He looks down at her, letting her rest on his chest as he leans against his car. "I can't lose you either," he pleads.

The softness is growing. Instead of just lingering, it is becoming all consuming. It takes all her energy to lift her hand and place it on his cheek. "Never," she says. "I love you."

Her hand drops, the last bit of energy fizzling out like a candle that burned late into the night.

As she drifts off, her lingering thought is of Ben, and the two of them lying together on the white sand, hand in hand, as the waves threaten to wash over them.

Chapter 48: Jordie

He spent most of the day sitting on the side of his bed with Brooke lying on top of it. They've barely spoken since the afternoon. There aren't a lot of words that come to mind when your girlfriend's dead father suddenly shows up at the door.

Brooke's pale complexation is even whiter than normal—almost translucent under the dim bedroom lighting. He tries to think of something to say to comfort her or something that could make light of the situation. Again, there's not a lot to say. "Congrats you're not a murderer," probably isn't going to be helpful either.

So, he did the only thing he could think of and took off, ready to race. Whether the cops came after him for his role with Jared, or Aaron found a new and twisted way to make his life living hell, it wouldn't matter while he was racing.

Ryder and Natalie are talking near Ryder's Supra. He

doesn't see Amanda, and as much as he wants to ask about it, he needs the instant adrenaline release.

"Race me," he says, no other pretense involved.

Ryder raises his head and watches him.

"Sure," he says, handing Natalie the drink he had in hand.

"You're not going to shit talk me first?" Jordie asks, half ready to pick a fight. He knows that he's the one who left Amanda, but part of him feels like Ryder's already won. He got the girl, and he got the life without constantly looking over his shoulder.

"Jordie, I think we both know you're in enough shit without me having to mock you," Ryder says.

Amanda, that bitch. She had run off to Ryder and told him what? Everything? Of course she did. He's seething. It feels like even more of a betrayal.

"What did she tell you?" he asks, snarling.

Natalie places the drink on the bumper of a random car and comes up close to Jordie. "Listen, *pendejo*, Amanda hasn't had to tell us anything. People talk."

"And what are they saying?" he asks.

"Just that you lost an entire shipment to a cop and somehow aren't dead," Natalie says. "Maybe you should be by now."

"Nat," Ryder says, holding his hand up like a warning. "That's enough."

"Enough of what?" she says, her Spanish accent thicker than usual. "I'm sick of this cabrón running around acting like he's a god."

"A god?" Jordie asks.

"Yes, like a *god*, always going on about how you're the best racer—about how Ryder is so jealous of your amazing skills, and how you're so fantastic when you're too stupid to even figure out how to keep drugs away from the cops."

He lunges forward, not sure what he's going to do, but fully ready to snap. Ryder pushes Natalie aside and comes inches from his face.

"What are you going to do, Vodheo?" Ryder asks.

But Jordie doesn't get a chance to respond. He's not sure what he would have done anyways. Not hit her, he thinks… probably. Even with his lapse of judgement, he's reasonably sure he wouldn't hit a woman. A hand taps Ryder on the shoulder, beckoning him to move. He does, and before Jordie can see who it is, he feels a fist slam into his nose, possibly crushing it as all he can feel is a wham and then an explosion of pain, blood raining from his nostrils as he tries to regain his footing.

"If you ever get close to her again, I'm going to break a lot more than your fucking nose," Ben screams at him.

He's still dizzy and can't see well enough, but he's sure that the crowd is staring at him.

Even though he's in pain, something occurs to him. "You're working for *Aaron*, aren't you?" he says, spitting out the blood that had run down to his mouth.

Ben seems startled by the name, stepping back. "I know *an* Aaron, why?" he asks, taken aback.

"Did you know that he's Brooke's father?" he screams at Ben.

From the smug grin on Ben's face, he's sure that he did.

"You think this is funny?" Jordie spits.

Ryder, having stepped back, seems perfectly fine with letting Ben and Jordie hash out whatever they need to, but he notices Natalie looks ready to fight too and is just as charged up as he is.

"Who is *Aaron?*" she asks.

"Who cares," Ryder interjects. "Just let them fight it out and walk away, Nat."

"Nat, he's right, this has nothing to do with you," Ben says, caressing her arm briefly before pulling away.

"Don't treat me like I'm made of porcelain! I'm staying," Natalie says adamantly.

Through all of the drama, and particularly through the pain of his nose, he hadn't seen Amanda approach.

"Brooke's father… is alive?" Amanda asks.

Natalie looks to her and asks, "Why do *you* care about Brooke's father?"

Ryder, more interested than before, turns to Amanda too. The crowd had moved on to follow the race between a Mustang and Porsche, probably two kids wanting to race their daddies cars. Luckily, the crowd is dispersing to watch.

"He works with Edge, the same place that Ben does. We thought he was dead."

He's surprised that Amanda hasn't spilled everything. Maybe he was wrong about her. Maybe part of her does still care about him. There's hope.

Ben laughs outright, "You mean you *hoped* he was dead.

Papa Brooke told me everything she did, right down to the way she was going to dispose of the body."

"Dispose of?" Natalie asks, and even Ryder seems aghast.

"Well, he's *not dead*, so it's over with," Jordie says. "But you knew he was up to something."

Amanda narrows her eyes, and everybody else follows suit.

"Is he actually that dumb?" Natalie asks, and Ryder nods, affirming with, "Apparently."

"What?" Jordie asks.

"Jordie," Amanda says, her voice calmer than everybody else's. "Attempted murder and being an accomplice are still crimes; you don't just get a clean slate because he happens to be alive."

On a logical level, he's sure that he knows that. But part of him was so stirred up with relief, remorse, and a tiny bit of reprieve, to believe that in some way his crimes were at the very least going to be less than they were. After all, Axel can't use Brooke against him anymore and neither can Jared. Still, he hadn't thought of the added repercussions. Dead men tell no tales.

"Fuck," he says, and the others just nod.

Chapter 49: Brooke

Her father sits across from her at the table. She has to blink more than usual because she's still not used to this. It's the second time she's seen Aaron since his resurrection. All of the guilt that she's suppressed for four years, all of the hate for killing a man who deserved it, they swirl around in her stomach and make her sick.

There's no rulebook on how to address the topic of trying to kill your father. Especially not when you wish he really was dead.

"What are you doing here?" she asks. He should have taken off across the world and started a new life. Left her behind and never came back. Instead, Aaron has to haunt her like the bastard he always was.

"Loose ends," he says.

She wonders briefly if he's going to kill her. An eye for an eye. He may have been an abusive asshole, but she wonders if that's cancelled out when you shoot somebody and then cart their body off with the mafia to bury or destroy the body in whatever way that they do.

"What does that mean?" she asks. She's too anxious to wait in suspense or play games. She just wants the answers forthright.

"I want to take down Jared," he says matter-of-factly. Like he's not a deluded idiot. If her killing him didn't take him out, she's sure this new plan will.

"That's absurd," she says. "Your 18-year-old daughter almost killed you."

He narrows his eyes, and his mouth moves into a snarl. "*Almost*," he says through clenched teeth.

In a way, she's glad her father is alive because without the guilt of how it ended, she can hate him again. She can hate him for every terrible thing that he's done in her life, for the childhood she could have had, and for the mafia she could have had nothing to do with. Without Aaron, she would be free of this life.

But in a way, if it weren't for that night, she wouldn't have Jordie either. She's not sure how she should feel about that realization.

She stands and walks around her kitchen. "I owe Jared a lot," she says, lying.

Aaron laughs audibly. "I know he screwed you—literally."

Her eyes widen. Hearing her should-be-dead father talk about her less than desirable sexual exploits is something she didn't need to check off her bucket list.

"That's not important," she says. "What's important is that he already wants Jordie dead because of the stupid cocaine he lost."

"About that," Aaron says. "I may have some *pertinent* information about that particular *acquisition*." Aaron always chose his words in an irritable fashion when he really wanted his victim to feel the weight of his statements. Even as an alcoholic father, he had found time to give her lectures in a fashion that rivalled great soliloquies.

Her search for answers had brought her very few. The fact that the key to figuring out at least some of the details about Jordie's excursion had laid in the empty coffin of her father. In a way, it's kind of poetic. If it weren't for her trying to kill her father, she wouldn't have been in bed with Jared in the first place—literally.

She stops pacing and leans against the counter, facing him to listen. "What do you know?" she asks.

"I know who called the *feds* in the first place," he says.

"Who?" she asks.

Aaron smiles an all-knowing smile and lets her stew in her thoughts for a moment before answering and says, "I did."

"You *what?*" she says, practically screaming.

"You shot me in the chest and left me to die," he says pointedly and clasps his hands together. Transaction finished.

"So, you then decided to set my boyfriend up to either die or be arrested?" she asks.

"As little as I care about Jordie, and as much as I'd love to see him suffer, that's not why I did it. I'm not going to waste my time on him without a reason," Aaron says. "You two are the ones that acted without a game plan."

"And what's the reason?" she asks, exasperated.

"I knew that Jared needed *the exact* shipment, or his customers would be pissed. Even that carload less was enough for Edge to step in and assure the buyers that his brother's oversight was *negligence*. The people Jordie was supposed to meet with were tycoons, and it was an important order; the timing mattered more than the other circumstances."

"So, what? You're leading a mafia coup-d'état?"

He shrugs. "Edge is the rightful leader, and he's less of a slimy bastard than Jared. Don't get me wrong, the man is absolutely deranged, but he has a code. Jared would shoot his own father if he had to—probably did," he says and adds as an afterthought, "Maybe that's where he got the idea to plant a gun in your hands."

"So, what are you saying? That I'm Jared?" she asks.

He shakes his head and says, "Nah. You're not cunning enough to be Jared. But you're certainly not innocent either."

She walks closer, sitting back at the table. She notices that Aaron doesn't smell like alcohol like he used to and that his white button-up shirt is clean. Apparently, her killing him is the best thing that ever happened to him.

"I'm not sorry," she says.

"Neither am I," he says as he nods. "But you want Jordie to live, right?"

She nods.

"Then you're stuck with me," he says. "For now, anyways."

"When this is over, are you going to return the favor and kill me?" she asks, perhaps too frankly, but she's exhausted, and she's unable to put up a façade.

"We'll see," he replies.

Chapter 50: Axel

Even as the years have gone by, he's never forgotten his first murder investigation. The first time he smelled blood on the scene as it started to harden to the floorboards. Thick puddles that were closer to brown as they welled together.

His second thought was about the victim's family. The weight and what it meant that the man on the floor was never going to go home again.

His next thought was that he'd hate to be the poor fucker that had to clean it up.

It doesn't matter how many times it happens. He still feels the weight against his skin. Seeing a young girl on the ground, being pulled out of the arms of the boy that loves her; he has to force himself not to be nauseated.

They chose to be here and be near these people. He can't be sure why. Are the few seconds of thrill that they feel behind the wheel truly worth it? Even then, lots of dumbasses street race and manage to stay away from criminal organizations.

He watches Ben, the intended target, as he paces the parking lot, bloodshot eyes and a temperament that threatened to boil over at any moment.

The stakes have been raised; he's not sure what to do next. Somebody wants to kill Ben for whatever reason.

Chapter 51: Brooke

24 Hours Ago

Sometimes, choices are hard. Other times, they're much easier than they should be. Aaron wanted her to help him take down Jared, and for what guarantee? So that Edge could take over the family business? Two psychopaths for the price of one? Not much of a sale.

So, she did the only thing that she could think of.

She went to the boss himself.

"You're sure he's alive?" Jared asks, visibly concerned. She's never seen Jared on edge before.

"Yes, he showed up at my apartment."

"Seriously? He's *that* bold?" Jared asks.

She nods and says, "Yep."

"How did he survive?" he asks.

"He said one of your men turned on you, that they were actually loyal to Edge. For a dead man, he talks a lot," she says.

Jared sighs and sits behind his desk. "Let me guess," he says, "Aaron was the one that told the feds about the supply route?"

She nods. "I don't think it was a coincidence that it happened when Jordie was the driver either," she says.

"Probably not," Jared replies, leaning back in his chair looking dismayed but also like he might burst out laughing.

"Why did he tell you this?" he asks.

"He wanted me to help him take you down in order to help Jordie get away from you," she says.

"And how would *that* work?" Jared asks.

"I guess there's no debts to be paid if you're dead," she says.

Jared's still leaning back and asks, "But you told me?"

"I shot my father in cold blood, and there's no way in hell that he's going to forgive me and Jordie. No matter what he says, he's still going to turn on me," she says.

"That's probably true," he says, folding his arms and moving the chair forward. "I'm guessing you want Jordie's debt cleared in exchange for this information?" he asks.

"I do," she says, "But I know that's not going to be so easy."

"Nothing ever is," he says, agreeing with her.

"What else do you want?" she asks.

"I can't let my brother get away with what he did," he says. "It's bad for business, and it's bad for morale."

"Uh-huh," she says, "Get to the point."

"You and Jordie spend a lot of time at the races, and I

know that Edge has drivers too. I want to know; who do you think his best runner is?"

"That's all you want?" she asks. "A name?"

He nods and gets up from the desk, walking towards her. "A driver for a driver. That's what's fair in business."

The only two drivers that work for Edge that she can think of are Andy and Ben. She could say no. Or she could make a decision. One or the other. If the cost is her and Jordie's freedom, she knows her answer.

It's not like she really gives a damn about any of the street racers that Jordie runs around with. Andy, though, was nice enough to offer her a soda once and seemed like a decent enough guy.

She doesn't hesitate before responding with, "Ben." Even though she knows what Jared is about to do.

Anything for her freedom.

"I want you to get Jordie and I out of the country," she says.

"That's a big ask," Jared says, close enough that she can smell his cologne.

"Whatever you do with Aaron, I don't want to be here for it. I know you gave me the gun hoping I'd take care of the problem. All I ask is to be gone this time. Do what you want with him," she says.

He nods, watching her closely. "I'll get you out of the country because you came to me," he says, and he leans in and kisses her cheek, then whispers in her ear, "but I'll miss you," before pulling away.

Despite their last encounter, she believes him and says,

"I'll miss you too, but this is for the best."

"I know," he says, almost somber.

"Jared?" she says before turning for the door.

"Yeah?" he asks.

"Thank you for being there when I needed you. As a teenager," she says. "I just wanted to know… Were you just using me to get what you wanted, or did part of you care?"

He sighs and holds his breath before shaking his head and answering, "If I didn't care, I don't think you and Jordie would still be alive."

"Thank you," she says and turns to leave, a small smile forming on her lips.

"You're welcome," he says as he shuts the door behind her.

Chapter 52: Ben

Edge and his men are gearing for war. He's too numb to worry about the carnage that might follow.

"You sure that bullet was meant for you?" Edge asks Ben.

They're in his office, the door closed for privacy. It's been two days since Natalie died. There is only one thing that Ben is sure of… Natalie stepped in front of him just as shots were fired.

The bullet was meant for him.

Because of him, the love of his life is being embalmed in some funeral home in the city.

"Yes, I'm sure," Ben says, resting his hands on his lap, the rest of his body completely still.

There's a knock on the door.

Edge hesitates for a moment, but he stands and opens it.

"Yes?" he asks, his voice raised slightly.

Another man walks in, pushing past Edge who grimaces

at the complete lack of respect. Ben's too numb to care about Edge's reaction.

"What do you want, Aaron?" Edge asks.

"I want to know when we're going to make the move on your brother," Aaron says.

Aaron is unshaven and wearing a dirty button up shirt.

"I'm pretty sure my brother just tried to have Ben here killed… which I'm not sure why since he's not even that important," Edge says.

Ben just stares at Edge.

"No offense, of course," Edge says and then turns his attention back to Aaron.

Natalie is dead, and it was supposed to be Ben. Nobody cares.

All of his losses have compounded. Everything he's done, every reaction to pain has been a domino effect.

Lost the baby, became a drug dealer, lost Natalie too.

Now what does he have left?

A mob war between two gangsters who clearly don't care if he dies. It's not like he can blame them; this war goes deeper than a couple street racers and low-brow drug runners.

Moving drugs was just quicker money for law-school. Getting "back on track" was just another domino falling.

Aaron's gaze turns to Ben, his eyes narrowing as he says, "I want to talk to you in private, Edge."

Edge shakes his head and says, "I think Ben's invested enough to be a part of this conversation."

As though Natalie was currency for a seat at the table.

Aaron almost growls as he says, "Fine."

He's not sure he wants to stay, but he's not ready to go home yet either, so he stays sitting. Edge and Aaron are both standing, towering over him, but he can't be bothered to stand up. His body feels like cement has been poured through his muscles. Time is passing slower—almost like there is a gray fog surrounding him.

"One of our boys on the inside has a schedule for Jared's warehouse meetings," Aaron tells Edge. "I think we should make the move; I just need your say-so."

Edge's hand gently moves to his beard. After a long minute of silence and contemplation, he finally says, "No, not yet."

"What are we waiting for?" Aaron demands.

"I don't need to explain myself to you," Edge says with a warning.

Aaron scowls, but he nods.

"Are you going to be okay, Ben?" Edge asks, adding, "I'm sorry about your girlfriend."

"No," Ben says, standing from the chair and moving toward the door. "But that doesn't matter."

Edge doesn't stop him from leaving. He walks out of the room and through the foyer, nothing concrete on his mind. He has nowhere to go. No one to go too.

Chapter 53: Amanda

It occurs to her as she sits in the pew of a rather large Catholic church that she had never discussed religion with Natalie. They had discussed every type of car, their engines, and the best places to acquire parts, but the topic of the afterlife or religious beliefs had never occurred to her.

Ryder is unmoving as he sits beside her. He hasn't said much in three days. She hasn't said much either. Even if she rarely shuts up, this is a moment that hasn't called for many words.

The local PD were all but helpful. They had no leads, and even if they might have known something, they were keeping their lips tight. A random act of gang violence possibly motivated by the illicit activities that Ms. Natalie Rodriquez was clearly associated with.

The question of her character seemed on the tip of their lips. Natalie was not a victim to them; she was just a bad Mexican girl that got too close to a bullet. Very sad. Nothing they could do.

Ryder's mother sits next to him, pale white skin like her own. She had introduced herself as Cecilia. She shook Amanda's hand despite their present surroundings and murmured that she wished they had met sooner under better pretenses. She then took the time to chastise Ryder for never introducing them. He simply nodded, too weak or too lost to come up with words. She seemed to have assumed that he and Amanda were a couple and neither had the energy to disagree.

Cecilia stirs often during the funeral. She seems discontent in the church pew, endlessly grabbing at the sleeves of her black dress.

Ryder still does not move, not even as his mother's eyes well up with tears. Amanda reaches across him to hand her a tissue. She had brought them dutifully after looking up on the internet, in a moment of haste, how people behave at Catholic funerals. Her own family had never discussed religion. Her father's family was Catholic once, but they had never attended church, and she hadn't known anybody close enough to attend a funeral.

Cecilia extends her hand, takes the tissues, and sheepishly smiles at her.

The preacher—or priest as she thinks they're called—mentions that the funeral will be a celebration of life, discarding the violent and horror-struck ending.

Her stomach churns. Something about celebrating the death of a 24-year-old doesn't sit right with her, but she remains seated. She's careful not to move too much because she doesn't want Ryder to see her discomfort.

She reaches out and clasps his hand. He barely squeezes it but faintly presses his thumb against her palm.

Nothing seems right as they watch quietly. Some of Natalie's family members give speeches, but Ryder does not. Even though he was likely the person that knew her best, he says nothing. Natalie was always the one to do the most talking between them, so Amanda understands his dilemma.

Perhaps Natalie would be of great help in this moment. She would know exactly what to say at her funeral. She would guide the conversation and cheer everybody up. Find a way to console those that were inconsolable and likely find a way to make everybody laugh.

But nobody is laughing. She can hear sniffles and the audible huff that comes when people have been crying for a prolonged period of time. She feels sluggish too, the weight of the room pressing against all her sides.

Scanning the audience is a good way to distract herself. She can't listen too closely to the sermon. She doesn't believe in anything the priest is saying, and worse, she doesn't want to come to the conclusion that heaven is some kind of penance for the weary. Instead, she's content to let anger boil under her skin. Natalie didn't die; she was murdered… and the reason is sitting in the second to last pew to the right.

She's surprised he showed up, clad in formal-wear, tie and all. It even looks like Ben had been crying. She grimaces, thinking that he has to be one of the dumbest people alive to think that he would be welcome here. But Natalie's family doesn't say anything or even seems to notice him. They should be outraged, but they are too focused on their grief to realize that its cause is in the room like a demon presiding over his work.

Of course she knows that Ben didn't pull the trigger, but whoever was gunning for him likely had a reason. Whatever guilt he feels, she's glad, and she hopes that it consumes him and tortures him until his final moment. She takes solace when she considers that while the Catholics are a little *too* preoccupied by heaven, they also propose a fitting solution for people like Ben. She hopes they're right and that he is awaiting a fate of fire and brimstone.

Another familiar face is in the pew behind Ben, and she's surprised to see him there. This time there's no ball cap, and he's wearing a black shirt, buttoned up completely.

Axel has attended the funeral which means that even though the cops weren't investigating, somebody cares. She resolves to meet him after the funeral, right before everybody leaves. She assumes, though, that he'd sneak out early so that he wouldn't have to explain his connection, or lack thereof, to the grieving family.

"Ryder, I'm going to get some air," she says.

He barely reacts but lets go of her hand. She feels shitty for leaving him, but she needs to get to Axel.

She gets out of the pew as quietly as she can and slinks out of the back door. No one is paying attention to her. It's an easy escape.

Chapter 54: Jordie

He's sure of very few things, but one of them is that Jared was responsible for the death of Natalie. He's sure that the intended target was not Natalie, a girl who didn't deserve it. If Jared is so callous with the lives of Ben and Natalie, he's utterly sure that his own life hangs in the balance.

But Brooke doesn't seem phased. She sits at the kitchen table doing her nails, painting them a deeply ironic red.

"What are you doing?" he asks.

She shrugs but doesn't move her hands, worried about chipping her nails. "I think it's abundantly clear what I'm doing."

"Natalie is dead," he says.

"Didn't really know her," Brooke says, seemingly unconcerned.

"What if it were you?" he asks, coming up beside her and

watching as she paints her nails. It's hard to fathom a world without her. For better or worse, they're blended together. Like an oil spill on the ocean.

"Then I'd be dead," she says, her face showing no emotion.

"Things are getting too deep. Jared…" He trails off because he can't handle where the thought is going. He always knew there was a risk of death, but now it's an inevitability.

"Jared is fine," Brooke says.

He notices their passports on the table, and his eyes widen. "What do you mean?" he asks slowly.

Brooke sighs, stands, and shakes her nails to help them dry faster. He notices that her hair is set back in a ponytail, and she's wearing jeans and sneakers. Ready to go.

"We're leaving," she says.

"We can't leave, I owe Jared money… and your father," he shakes his head. Everything is a mess.

She takes him by the hands, careful not to touch him with her nails, and looks up at him.

"Consider the debt *settled*," she says firmly.

"What?" he asks. There's no way in hell Jared would settle his debt just because she asked him to. "How?"

She rolls her eyes like she was never going to tell him. Making it perfectly clear that whatever happened, she wanted him to just follow along.

"I fixed your mess," she says. "Just barely."

"What's that supposed to mean?"

"I told Jared everything about Aaron and his lucrative

plan to get Jared killed or arrested. He was very generous in return," she says.

He shakes his head, not buying it. Not that her news seems untrue, but that can't be all. Especially not as things are heating up.

"What did you do?" he says, a little louder this time, letting go of her hands and pulling back.

She breathes deeply, then says something that she can never take back. "Jared asked me for a name of one of Edge's drivers."

"Wait," he says. "You *chose* Ben?"

She nods, not seeming too phased by the entire ordeal. "It was either him or Andy."

"You're standing here telling me that you chose a man to die, all so that we could, what? Trade our freedom?" he asks.

"Not ours, yours," she says. "It's not me that Jared wanted dead."

He turns his back to her, facing the kitchen wall. Trying to gather his thoughts about the woman who he's chosen to live the rest of his life with. He has to swallow his breath to keep his emotions, specifically anger, in check.

"I don't see why you're upset," she says. "Because of Aaron and Edge, your car got apprehended in the first place."

He practically growls his response, "Yeah, Aaron and Edge. Not Ben, and for sure not Natalie who was completely innocent."

"Nobody's innocent," she says.

"Yeah, the girl who shot her father would fucking know," he says in response a little too loudly.

She walks around him to be face to face, but he turns his head from her. The last thing he wants to do is look into her green eyes and be told how this was all for *him*.

But he knows it was for him. Just like every wrong choice he's made in the past four years was for her.

"I don't want to lose you," she says, her voice lower than it was before. "I would trade any other person for you. All of them."

He cups his hand over his mouth to cover the gaping. He tries to think things through.

"What are we going to do now?" she asks.

He shakes his head, unable to come up with an audible answer. How can he decide what to do next when he's not even sure that the woman he loves has any shred of humanity?

He lowers his hand and turns his head to look at her. The girl he fell for was innocent, even after what she did. He had seen a victim cowering in the corner, covered in the blood of the man that lay on the floor before her.

Everything that they were had hinged upon the fact that

Brooke was the victim to Aaron's wrath.

Now, he's faced with a harsher truth. Even if Aaron had been a catalyst, what if the girl he loves was never really a victim at all? Yes, Aaron had abused her, but she still pulled the trigger. Instead of the cops, she had insisted on Jared; every moment was tied to her choices.

"Did you *love* Jared?" he asks.

She shakes her head, aghast. "What the hell, Jordie?"

Her response is a little too quick and certainly too abrasive.

He asks again, "Did you love Jared?"

"I can't see how that matters," she says. "But no, I don't love Jared."

He rolls his eyes. It's enough of an answer, but it's certainly not what he wanted to hear.

"You always run to him and his world. You even let me get involved. If it weren't for you, he wouldn't have been at the races or seen me drive," his hands are shaking.

"I didn't force you to accept his offer," she says.

"No," he agrees. "But even now you keep running to him."

"I only ran to him because it was the best way to save you," she says. "If I hadn't exploited that relationship, it wouldn't be Natalie in a coffin."

"I'm not going to thank you for a 24-year-old being buried!" he yells. "Have some dignity."

She places her hand on his cheek, and he pushes it away. Her hands feel like sandpaper, and he just wants to get away from her.

"Jordie, I would do anything for you," she says, trying to make her voice sound soothing, but he just thinks of the distorted horror movie voices.

"No, you'd do anything for you," he says as he grabs his keys and takes off for the door, slamming it behind him. Not even stopping as she follows him, still calling for him to come back.

He gets in his car and just drives. No destination in mind. Just anywhere but in the apartment with his *femme fatale* girlfriend.

Chapter 55: Axel

As he turns the corner to leave the funeral, Amanda stands alone, waiting for him, stopping him in his tracks.

He probably shouldn't have been there at all, but the weight of being unable to stop the violence, even if it was unpredictable, has been keeping him awake at night.

"She was my friend," Amanda says, before he can ask. "We went to college together."

"I'm sorry," he says, and he truly is. He's sorry for all of the violence. Even if Natalie Rodriguez had decided to street race, she didn't deserve what happened.

Amanda leans against the building, looking weary. Her usual glow and energy are replaced with a solemnness that suits the occasion.

She tilts her head just enough to show she's heard him, but she doesn't say anything.

"Were you waiting for me?" he asks. "I saw you leave."

She nods, this time taking the time to do so.

"Why?" he asks.

"I don't know," she says. "I thought maybe you would know something."

He shakes his head. He knows that the attack was motivated by the mob and that it was likely a territory issue, but there are no answers that explain the magnitude of the situation. All he can do is place his hand on her shoulder, voice soft as he says, "I'm doing my best."

"I meant to tell you sooner," Amanda says, biting her lip in between words as she hesitates.

"Yes?" he asks.

"Aaron is alive; Brooke's father who she apparently thought she killed." Amanda sighs at the last part, her brow creasing, showing her complete distaste for Brooke.

He has to admit, it's an interesting piece of information. He's not sure how it all fits together, but it's likely important. "How do you know?" he asks.

"*Jordie* kind of freaked out at a race last week and told everybody. He's also pretty stupid because he doesn't realize that even trying to kill somebody is a crime," she says.

Axel half laughs, half sighs. It's not like he's surprised. "I'm more concerned with this Aaron thing than with Jordie and Brooke," he says even though he'd love to arrest all of them.

"I figured you would be," Amanda says. "It's also clear that the bullets were meant for Ben, right?" she asks.

Not that he should be discussing the case with a civilian,

but he nods anyways, pulling out sunglasses from his pocket and putting them on. It's hot, and the sun is piercing.

"Amanda, you need to stay away from these people," he says. "Things are only going to get worse, and I don't think driving a car is really worth the risk. Why don't you ask your dad to take you to the track?"

Her eyes widen a bit. "You know who I am?" she asks.

"I make a habit of checking up on the people that show up at my hotel room uninvited, especially whilst I'm under-cover."

The sound of singing inside the church signals the end of the mass. Their conversation is about to be cut short, but he feels the need to protect her. Not that there's much he can do. He thinks about the stray bullets and how any one of them could have hit her, and he feels sick to his stomach.

"Promise me you'll stay away from the races," he says.

"I can't do that."

He groans. "And why is that?"

"Because this was important to Natalie and to Ryder, and he's lost right now. So, if he's going to go, I'm going to be there for him."

"And what if the violence gets worse?" he asks, his voice tense because he's a bit infuriated by her insolence.

"We'll be careful. There's always bullets flying in Chicago, right?"

He narrows his eyes even though she can't see them under his aviators. "Just be careful."

"I will," she says, and their conversation is broken up when the doors of the church open, and the family comes out, all lined up next to the coffin.

Amanda nods at him before she finds Ryder and wraps her arm in his like they're coiled together.

He wonders briefly how serious their relationship is and if they're together or not.

Chapter 56: Ryder

He's not sure who to blame for Natalie's death. Ben is the obvious choice, but Natalie made her own decisions, and he knows she was incapable of being forced into anything.

Street racing was supposed to be fun. A release from the world around them. It was about the cars, the fun. Except now their spot has been taken over by gangsters playing sides, using the illegal drivers as assets to criminal organizations.

He just wants to race. He wants to feel his foot hit the peddle and the car accelerate beneath him. The shaking as the car springs forward has always put things into perspective—but nobody seems to want to race right now. Gun shots tend to dissipate a crowd.

He's standing in his yard. The cops had released the Chevelle to him, though he had the car towed home at his own cost.

The empty house he can almost deal with—spaces that used to be filled with Natalie. He can shut her bedroom door and pretend that she's busy with coursework, but the Chevelle—sitting outside unused, her motor painfully quiet—just seems wrong.

He should be angrier, out vying for revenge or screaming at the top of his lungs. Instead, he just feels a strange hollow sensation. All revenge would do is cause more pain.

Natalie didn't deserve what happened to her, and maybe he should blame Ben for the guns being there, but those stray bullets could have hit anybody. Even him.

So instead, he keeps staring at the Chevelle; the empty car that reminds him that his best friend is no longer around. He tries to choke back a tear. His palms move forward, pressing them against the hood of the car.

For the first time since Natalie died, he cries. He cries so hard that he coughs and has to struggle for a breath—the tears stinging his eyes and turning his face red, the salt causing a searing sensation on his skin.

Maybe it was her love for cars that killed her, or maybe it was her love for Ben. Maybe it was pain that could never be mended. Or maybe Natalie died because she was in the wrong place at the wrong time. No rhyme or reason, just another dead body on the streets of Chicago. Case-closed.

There's nowhere to channel his anger that's productive. Nothing he does will bring Natalie back to his family. All there's left to do is live with the pain.

Chapter 57: Brooke

A rapping noise on the door rouses her from her trance. She had been lying on the gray futon in the living room, staring at the beige carpet for hours since Jordie left.

She hadn't expected him to react so angrily—which is probably part of the problem. At some point she had lost herself, lost sight of what mattered. The only person worth doing anything for, Jordie, probably hates her.

She stands, wondering if it's Jordie at the door. It's strange he would knock on the door to his own apartment, but perhaps he wants to apologize and doesn't want to walk in on her without some formalities.

The door pushes in with a bang—clearly not Jordie at the door. Instead, it's the source of all her problems.

Aaron's jaw looks crooked, formed into a pissed off and menacing position. "What did you do?" he demands, voice rough.

"I didn't do anything," she says, unwavering.

She didn't. All she did was say a name, speak some words. If Aaron didn't want to piss off Jared, then perhaps he shouldn't have tried to undermine him *twice*.

He moves toward her quickly, not bothering to shut the door. His eyes spark with anger, and he spits as he growls his words, "You told Jared, didn't you?" he demands.

She purses her lips, not answering.

She wonders how he knows, but it's the least important factor. In the flicker of a second, she's back to her 18-year-old self—flashes of blood on her hands, shaking and crying for hours. The fear and the trembling come back to her.

This is why she and Jordie should have already been on a plane. She had even briefly thought about leaving without him, but she couldn't bring herself to.

"I knew you were Jared's slut, but I didn't think you were his whore too," he says, spitting on her as he talks.

Like cologne, she smells a whiff of the strong alcohol on his breath; his drink of choice, rum.

"Did you expect me to side with you?" she asks.

He stumbles forward, placing his hands on her shoulders and holding her in place, his grip too rough, but she doesn't move for fear of what he might do.

"I expected you to show some loyalty," he says, slurring just a bit on the word loyalty.

She thinks that it's a bit off that Aaron would expect her to remain loyal to a man that she shot, but she doesn't say it for risk of provoking him further. Instead, she nods, hoping that he takes it for some form of regret.

He grabs her by the hair, pulling her upwards so that her feet almost leave the carpet. She gasps from the sudden surge of pain, her scalp burning.

"I should have thrown you on the street when your mother left," he says, spitting on her face as he speaks.

She hasn't seen her mother in years, but she's sure that her reasons for leaving, even leaving her behind, were rooted in the abusive alcoholic who's still holding her up.

Letting go of her hair, he drops her but lands a kick on her stomach, knocking her to the floor. All she can feel is the pain that courses through her, like she's been hit by the full weight of a freight train. Her eyes water from the impact of the blow, and her arms reach out to hold the area.

"What, you're crying now?" he says, his tone mocking her. "Where's the *badass* with the gun now?" he asks, laughing.

She coughs, trying to get her breath. Even if she could, there's not a lot that she could say.

"You should have made sure I was dead when you had the chance," he says, kicking her once more, and she hears a crunch.

She screams in agony from the pain, sure that at least one of her ribs must have been broken, if not more. The ripples of pain keep flowing through her, coursing like waves in a violent storm.

Aaron's next hit lands on her shoulder, nearly knocking it out of place as she tries to cover her middle from his attack.

She's too weak to attempt to stand. She coughs, spitting blood on the carpet.

Aaron stands back to look at her, watching his handi-work as though it's one of his greatest achievements, even smiling.

"You're lucky I didn't do worse," he says. "You deserved it."

Aaron laughs at her, watching her cower on the floor, still whimpering in pain. Hot tears fall down her cheeks.

"You're useless, and all you bring is pain and suffering. Look at you there… weak, cowering," he says and then laughs again, shaking his head at her.

"You think you're tough," he continues, "but you always get Jared to do your dirty work."

He spits on her and leaves her on the floor of the apartment, alone and still shaking with pain.

Chapter 58: Axel

Axel and Jonny sit inside a pizza place eating slices, not because he's undercover, but because he's been craving pizza all week.

"They've gone quiet for now. I'm not sure what they're planning, but they're so quiet," he says, wiping the corner of his mouth with a napkin.

Jonny shrugs. "Sometimes they go quiet. Just be thankful for the break," he says.

Axel sighs, setting the napkin on the linoleum table and says, "I don't know, I'm more worried about the quiet. Something's brewing."

"This isn't the Ides of March; I'm sure one of them will make a move soon enough," Jonny says, and then he slurps from his giant soda.

"It's just bothering me. We still don't know who killed Natalie Rodriguez."

Jonny shrugs again, then takes another bite of his pizza.

"What should we be doing?" Axel asks.

Jonny puts down the pizza, "Why are you so caught up on Rodriguez?"

"I told somebody that I'd find out who did this," Axel says, thinking about Amanda.

"The pretty blonde?" Jonny asks, and Axel nods, but it's not about anything sexual. He considers how it could just as easily have been her shot in all this senseless violence. The thought makes him shake.

"I know she's just one girl, but there'll be more victims soon. There always are," Axel says, and Jonny bobs his head, content to keep eating the pizza.

"Are you listening to me?" he asks, and Jonny again nods. "Jonny?"

"What?" Jonny asks, stirring.

"What's going on with you?" Axel asks.

Jonny shakes his head, putting down the pizza. "I don't know," he says. "I'm just tired of the mafia crap. I should have just bought a bar."

"If you bought a bar, you'd bankrupt it by drinking all of the stores," he says.

"I'd rather be a bankrupt bar owner than an FBI agent," Jonny says, and Axel laughs.

"It's a mess," Axel says, thinking about how likely it is that he'll be discovered and killed.

"I could still get out and buy a bar," Jonny says.

"Can I come?" Axel asks.

"Yep," Jonny replies. "We can go to LA."

"Isn't that where your ex-wife is?" Axel asks, but he does consider the appeal of going home. Finally throwing in the towel and admitting enough is enough.

"It's a big city," Jonny says.

"True," Axel replies, and he considers what it would mean if they really did take off. "Too bad we can't..." he says.

"Too bad," Jonny agrees.

Chapter 59: Brooke

Jordie should have been home hours ago, but she continues to lie on the floor, clasping at her stomach, tears flowing from her eyes and mixing with the dirt and blood on the floor. It's unlikely she'll get her damage deposit back considering the state of the carpeting. Aaron could have at least taken off his muddy boots.

She tries to lift herself off the floor, but the pain stings so deep that she falls back to the carpet, nearly knocking her head on the leg of the coffee table in the process.

Slowly and through bone-shattering pain, she crawls toward the couch on her elbows, trying to prop up her middle so that her ribs won't grind, but it doesn't matter; the pain spreads. Nearly screaming, she finally reaches the couch and stretches enough to grab her cellphone and pulls it towards her.

She tells the phone to dial Jordie, but he doesn't answer.

She tries a second and a third time, but it goes straight to voicemail. She could call 911, but explaining that the man she tried to murder had beaten her up, all because of a mafia plot, seems a little inappropriate.

Then there was Jared. She tries to dial, but he doesn't answer either. She leans back, propped against the couch, spinning from the weight of her actions. In that moment, she has to face facts—she doesn't have a lot of friends.

If she won't go to a hospital, she's not sure what other options are left for her. The pain is clouding her judgment, and she's not sure how much longer she can stay conscious. So, she texts the last person who will ever help, giving her address and the words "HELP PLEASE" and hopes for the best.

Within seconds, her head falls back into the couch, too exhausted from the pain.

***

"Brooke? Are you okay?" Amanda asks, shaking her slightly. "What happened?"

Brooke wakes slowly, startled to see Amanda before she feels a searing pain and remembers.

"My father," she says through broken speech, having trouble talking through the rib pain.

Amanda gets down to her level and takes her by the arms, helping her to get up and reach the couch slowly, carefully helping her lie down.

"You need a doctor," she says, her eyes moving up and down Brooke to evaluate the damage. "Why didn't you call an ambulance?"

Brooke coughs and wheezes for a moment, struggling to answer. "Cops," she replies quickly.

"I don't know what you expect me to do or why you even called me," Amanda says, then she sighs before she says, "You never call the *right* person for help, do you? This is ridiculous. I'm *taking* you to the hospital."

"I had no one else," Brooke says through clenched teeth, then adds, "I don't want to go to the hospital."

Amanda ignores her and lifts her once more from the couch, barely able to move Brooke's weight. Brooke stops fighting it and stands, leaning against Amanda's arm. Like it or not, Brooke is going to the hospital.

Brooke's eyes are glassy from her fatigue. They are focused on Amanda. "I'm sorry," she says as they walk toward the hallway and the stairs. Of course, there's no elevator.

"What?" Amanda asks.

"I'm sorry," Brooke says again.

Amanda shakes her head. "There'll be plenty of time for that later. Right now, we need to get you medical attention."

"I'll be fine," Brooke says, groaning as she talks. "Besides, I deserve this."

Amanda doesn't respond.

"If I had never stolen Jordie from you, none of this would have happened," Brooke says.

Amanda can't help but laugh, especially in their present circumstances.

"What?" Brooke says, seemingly bewildered.

"You didn't *steal* Jordie. It took me a while to realize that, but if he was going to leave, he was going to leave no matter what."

Brooke nods, "I guess so, but still, the way it all happened."

"You mean thinking you killed your father and then making him help you bury your secret?" Amanda says, her voice sharp.

"Yeah," Brooke says, "that."

"It doesn't matter now," Amanda says and continues to lead Brooke to the WRX and puts her in the passenger seat, closing the door behind her.

Chapter 60: Amanda

According to the doctor, Brooke had two broken ribs, but with rest and some mild painkillers, she'd be fine. It was a quiet trip from the hospital. Brooke was loopy from the medication they gave her. The doctor, assuming Amanda and Brooke were friends, gave Amanda a prescription for pills to pick up and said she could have one more that night if the pain persisted. Amanda paid for the pills out of her own pocket and drove Brooke home, practically dragging her back up the stairs and planting her on the couch. By the time they got back, it was 4 am, an entire five hours since Brooke had called.

Amanda grabs the pills and a water bottle from the counter, bringing them both to Brooke. She gently puts the pill to Brooke's mouth—seeing she is still having trouble moving—and Brooke swallows both the pill and the water without complaint.

Amanda places the items on the small, chipped end table and cups her hands over her face, trying to figure out a solution.

Brooke's eyes are glassy from her fatigue.

"Why are you here? Are you here to get revenge?" Brooke asks.

Brooke coughs, and her eyes take a few seconds to focus on Amanda.

She shakes her head and takes Brooke's hand. "Revenge for what? I already told you, I'm over you taking Jordie from me."

Brooke shakes her head, and Amanda notices her dilated pupils.

"Not for that," she says, "because Natalie is dead."

"Natalie was shot because the mob was after Ben, not because of you," Amanda says, voice shaky.

Brooke nods and has to cough to speak, the pain in her ribs still getting the better of her. "Yes, but I *gave* them Ben's name."

"You what?" Amanda says, aghast.

Brooke bites her lip like she's feeling some kind of real emotions close to regret. "I'm sorry," she says.

"Sorry?" Amanda says, spitting. "You're fucking *sorry?*"

Brooke, so small on the couch, looks like an innocent victim, not like the sociopath that she obviously is.

"Why?" she asks. Even though no reason could come close to justification, she has to know.

"Jordie," Brooke says. "It's always for Jordie."

"You wanted Jared to let him go. So, you picked a name.

You traded another life for Jordie's—for his mistake," her entire body is shaking from the news. "How could you?!" Amanda screams.

Her voice low, maybe from guilt or the broken ribs, Brooke says, "I'd do anything for him."

"I believe that," Amanda says, lowering her voice and adding, "but that's not love… That's sick."

"Jared was going to kill him. You used to love him. What would you have done for him?" she asks.

"I would have talked to the cops or the feds! I would have let people who are grown-ups handle the situation! I wouldn't have…" She stops for a moment to take a breath, completely at odds. "Never this!"

"And if you talked? They'd kill you too," Brooke says, and Amanda wonders how true this is considering her connection to Axel.

"No, they would have protected you," she says.

Brooke laughs involuntarily, then winces in pain and says, "You think you're smarter than Jordie and me, but if you believe that, you're the dumbest of us all."

"Whatever," Amanda says, throwing the bottle of pills at her. "Do me a favour, and take them all," she says, then grabs her purse and leaves the apartment, slamming the door behind her.

Chapter 61: Jordie

No matter his choice, there's no clean exit from the situation he's in. He'd never admit it out loud, but for a brief moment, he had considered Brooke's offer to get away from it all—to leave their lives behind and start anew. They could take off to some foreign destination and sip cocktails on the beach instead of owning up to their mistakes.

No matter how much he tries to justify his actions, or Brooke's, they were wrong. Even if all he wanted to do was drive, and even if he'd never meant for anybody to get hurt, he knows that he played a part, and a large one at that.

"How long am I looking at?" he asks.

Axel, sitting across from him in the grey office, shrugs. "That depends on how much you give *us,*" he says. "They don't just offer pleas to drug runners for the hell of it, and you're dealing with a dangerous organization."

"I'll tell you whatever you want to know," he says, "but I need to know that I'll be okay."

"What do you know?" Axel asks.

Jordie sighs and looks Axel in the eyes. For a fed, he's not the worst guy he's ever met, and he can probably trust him.

"I know *several* of Jared's supply routes, and I'm willing to give them to you."

"I want to know who killed Natalie Rodriguez," Axel says.

"I don't know who," Jordie says, truthfully.

"Okay," Axel says, "but how does your girlfriend's father play into all of this?"

"Aaron worked under Jared's father, Lorenzo, who died. Jared ended up in charge, but Aaron wanted to take him down," Jordie says, feeling a bit suffocated by the gray of the room. If he can't handle the FBI holding cell, he's not sure how he'll handle federal prison.

"And Ben?"

"It could have been any driver or dealer. It was revenge for you apprehending me."

Axel seems pained by his answer, wincing visibly as Jordie speaks.

"If it could have been any of them, why Ben?"

He may want to tell the truth, but there are certain lines he can't cross. For better or worse, he still loves Brooke. Sure, she's capable of murder—and picking the name of a person to die—but he can't betray her on that level.

"It's not hard to know Ben is a driver for Edge. He's pretty open about it. Not exactly discreet."

Axel bobs his head; even if he's not buying it, he's accepting the answer.

"You helped traffic drugs and illegally street race, Jordie. Not to mention your dealings with a criminal organization," Axel says with a sigh. "But I'll do everything I can to get you a reduced sentence and keep you safe. You may be an idiot, but I don't think you're violent. Not like these guys you're entangled with."

He swallows his breath. It's the best answer he could hope for—apart from going on the run, and running from what? The most dangerous person he could think of, Brooke, would be there with him.

Chapter 62: Axel

Jordie Vodheo is finally sitting in the interrogation room of the Chicago bureau office—the young man who started it all, whose mere existence was enough to punish Axel with this crappy appointment.

He was supposed to be tracking drug shipments down the coast. Now, instead, he's been babysitting street racers. Watching the petty drama and these children throw their lives on the line.

Four months ago, he was tracking a particular shipment. It was smaller than most. Only $200,000 worth of cocaine. A miniscule amount considering the millions of dollars constantly moved back and forth.

Jordie was driving a Mercedes. Axel had him cornered in Florida. His intel was that Jordie was supposed to take the drugs to businessmen. His assumption was that Jared was trying to expand, show how good his shipments were. A little taste to get the nightclubs in Miami hooked.

Except Jordie never did make it to that meeting. An anonymous tip called in the car. Axel was waiting for the Mercedes just off the interstate. He finally tracked it down at a small motel. He was ready for the bust. He was geared up, ready to go inside the motel room and arrest Jordie. He called for backup; they were on their way.

When backup arrived, they finally stormed the motel room. Except it was empty. No Jordie, nobody. Turns out they had waited too long. Spooked the driver who had gone with the wind…

He did get the car, but how did he lose the kid? Where was Jordie hiding that he was able to get away from Axel?

He followed protocol and waited. In that time, Jordie managed to get away.

"How did you get away?" Axel asks Jordie who sits across from him.

"I saw you in the parking lot," Jordie says. "I was going to get a coke from the office, and I saw your same car that had tailed me before."

"You got away because you were thirsty?" Axel asks.

"When I saw you, I left the car there and I walked to a bus station, that's how I got back to Chicago."

"They think I let you go," Axel says, his hands scrunched into tight fists. It's not like he can blame those above him for thinking he was turned.

Putting him in Chicago, in the thick of it, is a good way to see if your agent has your best interests at heart. After all, he's bound to mess up if he's in the same city as the criminals he's screwing over.

Jordie shrugs and says, "Maybe you did by being so shit at your job."

Maybe he is shit at his job. So far, he's caught no criminals. Jordie came to him.

Chapter 63: Amanda

"Thanks for meeting me," Axel says to her as he opens the door to the new motel, having replaced the old one after having one too many unwanted guests. He ushers her in, closing the door firmly behind her. He then checks to assure the curtains are drawn. "Does anybody know you're here?" he asks.

"You're making this sound like a drug deal," she says and laughs half-heartedly, but she doesn't think any of it is funny. Not really.

I have something to tell you," he says, but he's talking slow, like he's testing his words. Not sure he should tell her what he's about to say.

"What?" she asks.

"Jordie confessed," he says. "To what, I'm not sure, but he's ready to talk, and we have him on trafficking. It's not *good.*"

He seems like he expects something of her. He waits for a reaction as she tries to compose herself, taking her purse and setting it down on the worn mahogany desk near folders that she assumes contain crime scene documents or whatever federal agents keep on their desks.

"So, what does that mean?" she asks, more composed than Axel expects because he steps backward for a moment, shakes his head, and then looks up at her.

"It means that he's going to do time."

"But he'll be alive?" Amanda asks.

"Yes," Axel says. "I believe we can keep him safe—probably get him as far away as possible, providing what he gives the agency is enough."

"Okay," Amanda says. She had expected much worse. Another body.

"Are you okay?" he asks her, stepping forward and carefully watching her. Like she's a china teacup that's just been knocked about, and he's wondering if she'll be chipped or shattered when she stops spinning.

"Yes," she says, and she means it. "I'm okay."

Federal agent or not, she's acutely aware of the smell of Axel's cologne and the way his collar is turned up, revealing his neck and the muscles that pour down to his chest.

She's been aware of several things since they met. The way he walks, confident and cool, even when he's supposed to be sulking around and pretending he's not important. It's impossible for him to hide it completely.

"How old are you?" she asks, suddenly aware that despite him seeming like a young agent—daunted and ready to act—he also holds himself like he's seen things, and his manner is certainly more refined than Ryder or Jordie's; not that it would take much to beat out the latter.

His eyebrow raises, but he replies with, "36," and she smiles at him.

"So, if you don't like to be called a cop, what do you prefer to be called?" she asks.

"Axel," he says a little too quickly, perhaps realizing he's gotten too personal without meaning to. "Uh, Special Agent Wariloe, I guess."

"And what's so special about you?" she asks, and she watches carefully to see how he reacts. If she challenged Jordie or Ryder, they'd be quick to retort.

Axel just shrugs. "Aside from completing the training, not much. Just a guy doing his job," he says.

"An incredibly important job," she says not so much mocking but playfully teasing.

"At your service," he says, and he tips a pretend hat. She laughs, not expecting this from him.

She sees, though, that he's being serious about it being a job. He may be caught up in this, but she doesn't think he has a hero complex.

She moves her eyes around the motel room. There are no personal artifacts. His clothes, which are tucked in the closet, are all neatly arranged, and aside from some candy bar wrappers in the trash and the files on the dresser, the room is dull. Even for a motel.

"How long has it been since you've seen your family or friends?" she asks, suddenly seeing Axel Wariloe as more than Agent Wariloe.

"I don't know," he says. "They live in California, so a while."

"My brother and sister are in California," she says, and she thinks of Jason and Jovie in Los Angeles, far away from her current mess. "I miss them too," she adds as an afterthought.

"It's so dry there this time of year," he says.

"I wouldn't know," she adds, and she wouldn't because every time Jason had asked, she'd refused to visit. Sure, she'd been to L.A., but usually in winter and for brief stints, never for longer than a weekend.

"Are you lonely?" she asks, but she can see it in his eyes, slated with gray, that he is.

He nods, though she sees his expression change like he's revealed too much—too many secrets that could burst and get him and those around him killed.

"Natalie's death isn't your fault," she says to him.

"I know that," he says.

"Do you really?" she asks and walks to the desk, opening the file to reveal the gruesome images that would have made her vomit, or at the very least shudder in pain, if she weren't numb from living through it in person. "Because it looks like you're obsessing."

"I'm doing my job," he says.

"I don't think it's your job to go to funerals in an unofficial capacity," she says. "Maybe it is, I don't know, but I doubt that's why."

"Are you trying to get a job at the bureau?" he asks her,

and she almost laughs, but the images of Natalie get the better of her, so she closes the file and tucks it under the others, turning to face Axel.

"I don't think I'm cut out for the pant suits. Way too *bleak*, and gray has never been my color."

"I think you could pull it off," he says, his mouth hanging open for a moment after, like he's not so sure what he said actually came out of his mouth.

"Hmm," she says, deliberating and taking a step closer to him. "I guess it all depends on the hemline. I'm afraid I might get lost in it, and it'll just look like a hazmat suit."

His eyes fix on her waist but move back to her eyes. "I've always said the uniforms could use some work; maybe some pink or fuchsia," he says, laughing at his own joke, trying to flip the power back to himself.

"Why did you join?" she asks him knowing it's too personal but curious about the man who had become Special Agent Axel Wariloe.

"I don't know," he says. "Why does anybody do anything?"

"They usually have a reason, some driving force that compels them."

He shrugs. "Why did you decide to street race?"

"Easy," she says. "I wanted to."

"Why can't that be my answer?" he asks, but he's smiling, not minding her grilling.

"Is it your answer?" she asks.

"I did want to," he says. "I wanted to have a purpose, though, too. Do some good. But I never liked red and blue."

"The local cops don't seem to be too competent anyways," she says, not having to feign her displeasure toward them.

"I won't argue," he says.

The weight of the room becomes different. There's an ease that replaces the formality of their former meetings. Instead of an agent, Axel has shown her something else, something human.

And the human that she sees, while he's attractive, painfully so, is also hurt. She is too, but there's something in Axel that seems to be seeking something, anything, that grounds him in the moment. Maybe adrenaline or that rush that comes when your life is on the line. He may think he occupies a different space to her, to the frivolity of street racing, but she can see that deep down he's lost.

Chapter 64: Axel

He's in the room with Jordie under the bright lights that are meant to make the suspect more susceptible, but after so many weeks in cheap motels, they're hurting his eyes too. Jordie's cleaning his fingernails with his thumb but doesn't seem particularly nervous.

"Something on your mind?" Axel asks, infuriated that this kid can try to act cool even when he's turned himself in.

"There's a race tonight. I wanted to be there," he says.

Axel rolls his eyes. These fucking kids and their racing. Didn't they have video games? Jesus, even he has a console. "Why can't you just play *Need for Speed* and smoke a joint like every other 24-year-old?"

"Nobody plays *Need for Speed* anymore," Jordie says, now crossing his arms like he's bored.

"You need to start talking if you want protection," Axel

says, tired of the games and ready to move on with his case once and for all.

"I want to know how my friends are. Will the other racers be implicated?"

Axel taps his pen on his folder, then sets it down. "By other racers, who do you mean?"

"Amanda, for starters. Do you think she's okay?"

"Didn't you two break up years ago?" Axel asks. The look of surprise on Jordie's face tells him that he's revealed a little more than he should have.

"We did," Jordie says. "Doesn't mean I don't care."

"She was fine when I saw her the other night," Axel says, and it's impossible to hide the smugness in his voice. Jordie pisses him off, and the other agents were scattered about thinking that Jordie was a complete waste of time and resource. They're probably right.

To Jordie's credit, his cheeks briefly turn red, having caught the implication. Axel's surprised. He figured Jordie was too dull to catch on.

"Isn't that against some kind of ethics code?" Jordie asks, his coolness finally wavering.

"Like what? Don't sleep with captivating blondes?" Jordie huffs.

"Oh, don't act so fucking pissed. It's not like you're good enough for her anyways. Your little murderess is much more your speed."

"Technically, the person she 'murdered' is alive," Jordie adds.

"A grievous oversight, I presume," Axel says, opening his

file and placing his evidence before Jordie. "I have the pieces; I just need you to give me more. Who killed Natalie Rodriguez, for starters?"

Jordie swallows his breath, hard.

Axel repeats the question.

"I don't know," Jordie says, and he doesn't seem to be lying, per se, but there's more information lingering under his words.

"Okay," Axel says, but he decides to re-frame the question. "You probably don't know who killed her exactly, but who called the hit?"

Jordie's eyes shift, landing on anything but Axel—the clock, the pen, the sound system.

"Jordie…"

Jordie shakes his head and speaks with the lowest voice he's heard from him. "If I tell you, there's no going back."

"Jordie, you're in FBI lock-up. You passed go and went straight to jail the second I got the car. Tell me."

"It's not going to matter," Jordie says, "They'll have covered their tracks."

"That's true," Axel says, "but at the very least I can say that you're cooperating."

"Jared was going to kill Ben for payback," Jordie says.

Axel nods and signals his hand for Jordie to go on.

"It was Brooke's father, Aaron, that alerted the FBI of our routes. He wants to take down Jared for good."

"Why Ben, though?" Axel asks, mostly concerned with Jordie's willingness to relay information.

Jordie chokes up, fakes a cough, and then shakes his

head. "It didn't matter. It just had to be any one of his runners. An eye for an eye. It could have been anybody."

"Nobody gave him a name?"

Jordie shakes his head, and his eyes reveal a clear lie, but he moves on. The kid had already started to shut down, and he's worried if he presses further, he won't get information that truly matters.

"Okay," Axel says, "you said Aaron wants to take out Jared. Do you know anything else?"

Jordie shakes his head. "No, but he showed up at the apartment. He tried to get Brooke to flip…"

"Ah," Axel says. He'd already pieced together who'd shared the name. Not that it was that hard of a conclusion to make. There were only two people that Jordie would protect, and he's pretty sure it wasn't Amanda that talked.

"Do you know where Aaron is now?" Axel asks.

"I don't know. His house? Planning to storm the castle with a brigade? I've told you what I know about this."

"You did, thank you," Axel says. "I'll be back."

He steps up from the chair and signals for two agents to take Jordie back to holding.

He thinks of the photos of Aaron's victims from his time working for Jared as a henchman in his file folder. All of the bodies that had been left mangled, destroyed, and weathered before their discovery. Jordie and Brooke might be pains in the ass, but Jared versus Aaron could have lethal consequences.

Chapter 65: Brooke

Her phone rings. She picks up without looking at the number and is only partially surprised when it's Jared on the other line.

"I heard what happened with your father," he says, his voice cool and not revealing anything about his current mood.

It still hurts to talk, but she manages to answer without her voice cracking too much, saying, "I tried to call you."

She can imagine him on the other end, crisp business suit, standing in his office by the window that overlooks a large oak tree.

"I know," he says. "I was busy."

"Okay," she says. Not sure what she expected. Nothing, probably. "So why did you call?"

"I called to tell you that it's over. I still have a way for you to get out of the country, but you have to leave first thing in the morning."

"Jordie isn't home yet," she says. She's still not sure where he is, and she's starting to worry. He's mad at her, but this is the longest they've gone without contact in years.

"He's not going with you," Jared says, "and you're lucky I'm still letting you go at all."

"What do you mean?" she asks, then winces from her pain. "What happened?"

"Jordie is in FBI custody. I don't know what he's said, but considering the drugs he already gave them, I'd imagine he'll serve time for trafficking. A lot of time."

She has to steady herself so that she doesn't drop the phone. "Can I come see you?" she asks.

"Brooke, I don't think you understand—your boyfriend is *with the feds.* You're never going to see me again."

"I had nothing to do with that!" she shouts as loud as the pain will allow.

"Brooke, you and Vodheo are liabilities. I made the mistake of letting our history cloud my judgement, but that's not going to happen again. There'll be a car for you in the morning. Get in it, leave, and never come back. That's not a request."

She sits silently, Jared breathing on the other end of the line for a moment before finally hanging up.

She stands, hands shaking, and pours herself a glass of whiskey; the irony of family alcoholism not lost on her. Jordie had gone to the feds. He's probably told on her too. For everything. Everything she had sacrificed for him, and for what?

She sips on her drink carefully, not wanting to aggravate her ribs further.

She makes a mental checklist of everything she should pack and what she should leave behind. She places her cup on the counter, careful not to let it clank, and walks to the closet that her and Jordie shared. A lot of the clothes are his. Crappy Abercrombie bullshit that he insisted on wearing. The dude has more clothes than her.

She turns, walks to the window, and opens it. There's no screen as it had broken the winter before, and their landlord never cared about updates. She walks back to the closet, wraps her arms around Jordie's preppy bullshit clothes, and picks them up all at once. Arms full, she takes them to the window and thrusts them to the ground. If he ever gets out of prison, the fucker can wander around naked.

Instead of packing her own clothes, she goes back to the kitchen and pours herself a double, sipping the malt liquor and weighing her lack of options carefully. She probably shouldn't be mixing it with the pain medication, but the fear of being sober with the knowledge of her world falling apart is too great.

It's likely that she'll never see Jordie again—whether he gets away or whether Jared has him murdered. He's signed himself to a life of confinement one way or another. Herself? She's not sure. Jared could be luring her to her own doom. In that situation, running would only piss him off more.

She could take Aaron up on his offer and just help kill Jared, but hydras never go down so easily. The solid choice is to sip back her drink and nurse another. If she's lucky, she'll still be drunk when the car gets there in the morning.

Chapter 66: Jordie

He didn't expect to be back in the investigation room so soon. He figured they'd let him stew, think about what he's done like it's detention. Maybe try to have time to think about all the horrors that Jared would inflict if they didn't offer their protection. A second agent is sitting next to him, this one with a southern drawl and a more relaxed look. Axel had referred to him as Agent Fonis.

"I don't know what else you want to know from me right now," Jordie says, rubbing his eyes. "The accommodation here is shit."

Axel looks different from usual. The guy's usually pretty high and mighty with his FBI shit, but he actually looks pretty somber for once.

"Jordie, I'm not here for more information right now," he says, and he's sitting up pin-straight, the way suits always do in TV shows.

"Oh?" he asks. "Did you get me a plea?"

Axel shakes his head, "No, that's not it."

Jordie shrugs, "Then can I go back and pretend to sleep on the concrete slab that you call a bed?"

"There was a 911 call from your apartment last night."

Jordie tries to spring up, but the handcuffs stop him. "What happened? Did Jared turn on her?"

"I don't think so," Axel says, still upright, all business.

"Then what?" Jordie asks impatiently.

Agent Fonis clears his throat and attempts sympathy, but with his southern accent, the condescension still rings in his voice. "I'm sorry, but your girlfriend passed away."

"The fuck does that mean?" Jordie asks, pulling at the cuffs with his hands.

"She was found on the street, face-down."

"What do you mean, on the street? Did somebody murder her?" Jordie asks, still in disbelief. This has to be a ploy, some way to get him to turn further. "This isn't going to work; I don't know what else to tell you—stop lying!"

"Jordie," Axel says, "we don't have all the facts, but there was a lot of alcohol found in her system as well as painkillers. She had broken ribs from before the fall, and it seems she might have fallen out the window."

"That doesn't make sense. We never open the window," he says, and they really haven't. Not since the screen broke. "Somebody must have pushed her. How was she found?"

Agent Fonis takes a deep breath; he's clearly here as some kind of emotional backup for Axel. He then clears his throat once more, prolonging speaking as long as he can.

"Just fucking tell me," Jordie says, the suspense making the news more cataclysmic than before.

"She was found face-down on the sidewalk, surrounded by men's clothing," Axel says, still deadpan serious despite the absurdity of the story.

"… What?" Jordie asks.

"It seems she had removed all of your clothes from the apartment and thrown them out the window. With the mix of painkillers and alcohol, it's possible at some point that she lost her balance and fell."

"She threw my clothes out…" he says, more of a statement than question. "All of them?"

The two agents nod.

"So, she knew I betrayed her."

"It's probable," Axel says.

"Do you think it was an accident?" Jordie asks, coming to a similar conclusion that the agents must have. "Or did she…?" he asks, gasping for air as he speaks.

"We're not sure. There was no note, but it's a possibility."

He thinks of Brooke lying there on the pavement. He thinks of all the atrocities they'd committed for each other. "This can't be it," he says. "It just can't be."

"I'm sorry," Axel says, but Jordie doesn't believe him. To Axel, Brooke is nothing more than a girl willing to kill to get what she wants. To him, she was everything.

"What's the point of it all?" he asks, not expecting an answer, but the two agents shake their heads anyways.

"I don't think there is one," Agent Fonis says.

"Sometimes life is just a series of stupid decisions until

one of them catches up to you," Axel says, and the other agent shoots him a look that shuts Axel up.

Axel shrugs his shoulders back, but Jordie's so preoccupied he only notices it in passing.

Chapter 67: Amanda

She got the news of Brooke's death at 11a.m. Axel had called. He had no answers as to how it had happened. It appeared to be a suicide. Pills and alcohol. Brooke, it seems, had taken her up on her offer after all. She thinks of her adversary on the ground, helpless, having fallen several storeys.

It's a kind of numbing realization.

Ryder had been colder than before, not really paying her much attention, and the funny thing is, she didn't seem to mind. The heat had gone away, replaced by a cool feeling. She wanted to race for the thrill, for the adrenaline, the charge—to feel alive.

Instead, all she found was death. Brooke, Natalie, and the imprisonment of Jordie.

By 1p.m., she had loaded her suitcase in her WRX along with the unpacked boxes of clothes. She left all of Natalie's parts there and a note for Ryder explaining that she quit. By all accounts, nobody had been hanging around their usual spots anyways, likely too spooked by the deaths and arrests.

Now, as the evening falls over the road on a relatively chilly fall evening, she's past state lines, still driving. She checks the GPS. She's 5 hours into a 29-hour drive, but she's not quite ready to rest yet.

She's not sure what she was looking for at the races. Perhaps it was some way to connect with her father or maybe to prove that she could do what she wanted. Her fingernails feel lighter on the steering wheel as she drives on the freeway, ready to find her next fix in the best place to reinvent yourself—Los Angeles.

Chapter 68: Ben

Lately, Ben's been playing the loyal little soldier role. Edge trusts him because he nearly took a bullet for "the cause", as he's called it. Ben says nothing. He arrives on time. He makes his runs, and he delivers the drugs to the dealers.

But Edge also wanted Ben to go places with Aaron who clearly hasn't wanted Ben there at all. Not that Ben cares.

Edge says where to go, and he goes.

Every day is more of the same. Ben does as he's told. He doesn't make waves. Drugs here, drugs there. It doesn't matter one bit if they're coming or going. Avoiding the cops is easy enough if you know what you're doing, and he's used to being on the streets. He knows what routes are filled with soccer moms who call and tell on suspicious vehicles, so he convinced Edge to let him drive one of their shitty mommy van-type SUVs. Smooth sailing, and Edge thinks he's a genius.

Aaron doesn't say much around Ben. He doesn't trust him. His eyes are always leering. When they're together in the vehicle, he makes Ben drive so that he can send text messages, rarely saying anything out loud.

Most of the time with Aaron is spent waiting. Aaron has his meetings in private buildings, usually offices, and Ben just waits in the SUV. He's careful not to play the music too loud. The less attention the better.

Currently, he's waiting for Aaron, the radio is on a low-setting, country music playing. He's not a fan, but he figures people expect country-music fans to be red-blooded, crime-free Americans or something like that.

He notices something curious. Aaron, who he can never tell is sober or drunk, had left his burner phone on the seat of the car.

Ben checks out the window, and his eyes scan the area for Aaron who has yet to return. The coast is clear. He picks up the phone; its keys are sticky. He grimaces but flips the screen open. Searching through the QWERTY style text messages requires an extra level of decoding, but he can make out one of the messages.

Shipment @ E Dock Fri 7.

Clearly Aaron isn't worried about coding his messages. Whomever he's talking to is likely sharing intel. As far as he knows, Edge doesn't get any shipments from docks. He uses an airfield.

This must be one of the shipments that Aaron and Edge were talking about. This shipment was Jared's.

Ben uses his own modern phone to quickly snap a photo and exits the messaging. He places the phone back where it was, stickiness and all in the seat.

Aaron takes another 10 minutes before he's back in the seat. He doesn't talk to Ben—rarely does, just keeps typing away on his ancient phone as they take off, and Ben drives him around like a chauffer.

On the entire drive, Aaron doesn't say much except, "Drop me off at my safehouse." He keeps referring to a trailer in a trailer park as a safe-house, but Ben's pretty sure that nobody gives a shit about Aaron's safety.

The entire drive, Ben is mulling over the war that's brewing between Edge and Jared. The war he never really signed up for that's already taken everything from him.

By the time he drops off Aaron and drives off, he's come to a conclusion. He stops the SUV on a tiny side road and gets out, making sure that he's away from the car in-case Edge or Aaron have bugged it.

He dials a number on his phone.

"FBI tip line," a lady says from the other end.

"I'd like to report a drug shipment," Ben says into the receiver.

Chapter 69: Axel

An anonymous tip brought Axel to a shipping warehouse at a dock known on their radar for ties to Jared's organization—although it's nothing they could prove definitively, at least not on paper. Aaron had met Jared there, and Jared showed irritation when Aaron had arrived instead of his supplier who could very well be dead considering the current circumstances.

Despite its criminal leanings, the warehouse is stark white and clean, something he'd expect of a military hanger. The shelves are metal and crisp with a brick enclave that leads to the few closed-off offices.

He's standing against the wall of the enclave, having only barely concealed himself after entering from a back entrance. Jared, who he had only seen from photographs, was surprisingly calm and collected for his position.; not only as the mob boss that had inherited a criminal empire from his father but also considering Aaron's gun was already raised and pointed at Jared.

Perhaps Jared was convinced that he could easily reach into the holster on his belt, but Aaron was smirking and assured Jared that by the time he reached for the gun, Jared would be dead.

"Then just kill me," Jared says with a sigh, like he has more important business to attend to.

Aaron's gun shakes a bit as he deliberates. "I'll kill you," he says. "Soon enough."

"What are you waiting for then?" Jared asks.

Aaron's phone buzzes, and he answers somebody on a Bluetooth device, then nods his head, pulling back the safety on his gun as he says, "Thanks," to the caller.

Whomever was on the other line had vital information. Aaron raises the gun to take a shot, and Axel steps forward, pressing his hand on the trigger of his gun, already raised in cover.

He pops off two shots, and Aaron moves, ducking and repositioning himself. Jared pulls his gun too and only briefly turns his attention to Axel before focusing on the fire fight. Aaron shoots twice more, narrowly missing Jared's chest.

Jonny was supposed to arrive with backup, and hopefully they're outside and ready to enter at any moment—but there was a good chance that he's alone.

Gun still raised, he switches his vision to the other men. Jared, wearing all Armani, and Aaron, disheveled like he just left the bar, in a dance. Aaron only tried to target Axel once and had turned his attention back to Jared when he missed, his shots revealing that he probably *did* just come from a bar.

Nonetheless, his gun raises, and his hand goes toward the trigger. Axel clicks the trigger on his gun, and Aaron's body jolts. He loses balance and falls to the floor of the warehouse moments later.

Jared steps beside him and looks down at Aaron, blood beginning to spill on the pristine white tile. "He's always been a mess," Jared says, shaking his head.

Axel turns to face Jared. He wasn't sure what he expected from him. By all accounts, Jared is a ruthless killer, a manipulative murderer. Yet, he nods his head at Axel.

"I wondered when we'd meet Agent Wariloe," he says.

"You know who I am?" Axel asks. He truly has the worst cover on earth—lack of cover that is.

Jared nods. "I did. I certainly expected a different ending when you nearly apprehended Jordie all those months ago. Still, I owe you."

"I suppose you do," Axel says. "But you know I'm going to try and arrest you eventually?"

"Not today, though," Jared says, assuredly.

The other agents had already informed him that the shipment was clean. It was a "legitimate" order of supplies for Jared's suspected front, a boat-selling business. The shipment was boat engines, and other than Aaron's gun, there's no crime here.

Aaron stirs, not dead but withering in pain from the wound; blood is pooling, but it's probably not likely to kill him. The sirens cut through the night outside, backup having arrived.

"I'll have to take a statement, but since I can't prove you did anything wrong other than be targeted by a known murderer, you can go after that," Axel says on edge because the man he's been tracking for months is standing in front of him, and he can't do anything about it except save the life of a man he knows is a threat.

Not only is his cover obliterated, but this is only the beginning.

Jared nods, "I suppose you're not going to tell me what happened with Jordie and that car?"

Axel shakes his head. "There's nothing to tell. I found the car. No driver."

Jared laughs and rolls his eyes before speaking again. "Jordie's stupid, but I can't imagine he's that stupid. Did you let him go?"

"No," Axel says. "and that's all I'm saying."

"The little bastard gave you the car, didn't he?" Jared says, but Jonny and the other agents come barreling in, guns raised.

Axel raises his hand, signaling that they're fine, and meets Jared's eyes, not saying anything. Just looking at him. Their eyes joined for only a few seconds, but Jared nods, the two reaching a brief understanding.

The paramedics attend to Aaron, and handcuffs are applied to the stretcher. Luckily for him and the justice system, Aaron was likely to make a full recovery. He mentally counts the bodies in his folder, all of the victims that would have justice. He has to push back the thought of how many more would be added to another folder, Jared's, as Jonny takes his statement.

Axel watches the two interact, both professional. Jared's about as shaken by the incident as a man who had just finished yoga.

The paramedics, escorted by two agents, take Aaron, and Jared walks out the front door. Like this never happened.

"You've got a win for once," Jonny says, clapping Axel on the back. "Congrats."

Axel nods, but his face betrays him.

"We have nothing to arrest him on right now," Jonny says.

"I could have let Aaron take the shot," Axel says to Jonny. "This would have been over."

"There'd still have been Edge and his goonies," Jonny says, but his grip tightens. "You did the right thing."

"Did I?" Axel asks. "Would you have done the same?"

Jonny lets go, and his mouth shifts to the side as he thinks. After a moment, he says, "I don't know. I hope so."

"What do you mean?"

"Letting Jared die might stop what's coming, but you still need to live in your skin when this is over."

"It's never going to be over," Axel says with a sigh. "Not any time soon."

Jonny says nothing, just nods in agreement and puts away the notepad he'd written Jared's statements on.

To be continued...

Shaylynn Hayes is a writer, graphic/web designer, political science enthusiast, and lover of flowers and the ocean. Shaylynn comes from Cape Breton Island, Nova Scotia, but has always been fascinated with  fast-paced, morally ambiguous stories. Some of her favourite books include *Savages* by Don Winslow, *Beautiful Disaster* by Jamie McGuire, and classics like *Wuthering Heights*, and *Pride and Prejudice*. Shaylynn also likes to take influence from television and loves shows like *Gossip Girl, 90210, Pretty Little Liars, Desperate Housewives, Dead To Me*, and really anything where character-driven mistakes cause drama. And of course, Shaylynn loves car films, with particular love for *The Fast and the Furious, Smokey and the Bandit*, and *Need for Speed*. Then there's the really bad street racing films (think b-list). She loves them too.